"Gibb's prose is elegant and sings with an almost Victorian delicacy and sophistication: Dickens, interrupted."
—*San Francisco Chronicle*

"An extraordinary Canadian talent. . . . The intricacy of Gibb's language transports you." —*The Edmonton Journal*

"Anger, honesty, compassion, fear, wit and insight electrify Gibb's deft sentences, singing the importance of belonging, of self-worth and of story." —*Winnipeg Free Press*

"Gibb's writing is laser-like." —*Toronto Star*

"A debunker of stereotypes and a seeker of the big picture, [Gibb] isn't satisfied with merely creating convincing characters and a bold plot. She educates and enlightens the reader."
—*Montreal Gazette*

"Gibb's thoughtful and intricate writing weaves an unforgettable portrait . . . and her observations of humanity make clear the similarities in all of us." —*The Seattlest*

PRAISE FOR *THIS IS HAPPY*

"A powerful testament to what people can overcome and permission for what people can't." —*Toronto Star*

"[Camilla Gibb is] a gifted storyteller. . . . Her story is touching, human, alive. . . . It is beautifully written, brave and sincere. Enjoy." —*Vancouver Sun*

"An array of life experiences both marvelous and painful in quiet language that often belies their extraordinariness. . . . *This Is Happy* is a tiny green shoot peeking through a crack in heavy concrete, wily and survivalist, but tenuous too." —*The Globe and Mail*

"*This Is Happy* has a rawness and power that's hard to resist. . . . Gibb's themes are important, and she has some powerful insights. . . . There's no doubt this engaging memoir comes from a gifted writer." —*NOW* (Toronto)

"A raw, exposed nerve sheathed in poetic insights. . . . Gibb's journey from 'there to here' is an honest and unflinching look at the pain of abandonment, and the deep digging and work you must undertake to rebuild your world and find your happiness." —CBC News

Also by Camilla Gibb

Mouthing the Words
The Petty Details of So-and-so's Life
Sweetness in the Belly
The Beauty of Humanity Movement
This Is Happy

THE
RELATIVES

A Novel

CAMILLA GIBB

ANCHOR CANADA

Anchor Canada paperback published 2023
Doubleday Canada hardcover published 2021

Library and Archives Canada Cataloguing in Publication
Title: The relatives / Camilla Gibb.
Names: Gibb, Camilla, author.
Identifiers: Canadiana 20200321536 | ISBN 9780385678117 (softcover)
Classification: LCC PS8563.I2437 R44 2022 | DDC C813/.54—dc23

Cover and book design: Lisa Jager
Cover and title-page art: AVNphotolab/Getty Images

Printed in the United States of America

Published in Canada by Anchor Canada,
a division of Penguin Random House Canada Limited,
a Penguin Random House company

www.penguinrandomhouse.ca

10 9 8 7 6 5 4 3 2 1

Penguin
Random House
ANCHOR CANADA

LILA

JACQUI PRESSES a manila file into my hands for the third time in four months. The label is simply marked "Robin." I know she thinks it will do me good to take the case on, but she also knows me well enough not to say it. We have been working together now for more than a decade—I interned here during my social work training and two years later, after my first job ended in disaster, Jacqui offered me an opportunity to redeem myself under her supervision. She is a mentor and a friend—I was even maid of honour at her wedding to Solomon, a second one for each of them, last year.

I slap the folder against my palm and smile. Jacqui knows I have run out of excuses.

Robin was referred to us in the spring by the Children's Aid Society, the way most children come into our services. Our team provides mental health assessment and treatment in cases where the police are involved. This case is a particular mystery. In April, the police found a girl wandering in her pyjamas in High Park. A dental exam suggested she was about eleven. She didn't speak then and hasn't spoken in the five months since. No one has reported her missing or come forward to claim her.

It was Jacqui who, after her initial psychiatric assessment, gave Robin her name. Jacqui would oversee the case, reporting back to Children's Aid, prescribing medication if necessary, and work in consultation with a social worker on an overall treatment plan. The social worker would be the one directly responsible for executing the plan, the front-line worker charged with the delicate work of establishing a relationship with Robin and liaising with the various parties involved.

When Jacqui first came to me with Robin's case, I was working with a young man who, after several months in a methadone program, had decided to lay charges against his former hockey coach. I knew he would need a lot of additional support once he went public with his story and insisted I couldn't take on another case when I needed to be available not only to him, but to any other former players who might come forward as a consequence. While this was true, and while I have seen many disturbing things over the years, what is even truer is that my reluctance to work with children has almost developed into an aversion.

Jacqui assigned another social worker to the case, at least for a time. When she approached me with the file again a couple of months later I said I would consider it, but then my mother, with her mild dementia and osteoporotic hips, fell down several flights of stairs in her building one early July morning. Why she was in the stairwell at all, I will never know—perhaps she never knew either. She smashed her head against the concrete landing and died of a brain haemorrhage shortly after.

It had all happened so suddenly that it wasn't until after the funeral that I really broke down. Jacqui was on call that weekend, and had received a page to go in to the hospital. Solomon came to help me clear the bigger pieces of furniture out of my mother's condo. He and I heaved and shifted a couch inch by inch into the service elevator, taking it down to the trash.

On subsequent weekends I went back alone to sort through her papers, clothes, the smaller things. Her bathrobe was still hanging behind her bedroom door. My mother was a complicated woman with dark moods and agoraphobic periods, but her bathrobe, still smelling of the lavender lotion she rubbed into her skin, was a remnant of the more tender part of her.

I lifted her bathrobe from the hook and put it on, the sleeves far too short, the belt running around my ribcage rather than my waist. I went into the kitchen then to make myself a cup of tea. The first cupboard I opened contained ten cans of Campbell's chicken noodle soup and a box of saltines. The second held the tea bags and a box of Sifto salt. I knew in that moment that I had to go back to AA.

I scheduled subsequent trips to her condo around meetings I never quite managed to get to. Every Saturday for weeks, all I did was go up to her unit and sit on the faded Persian rug. I couldn't bring myself to touch anything. Eventually I brought a bottle of vodka with me. I drank that entire thing, not even bothering with a glass. I passed out on the carpet, waking at some point in the middle of the night, not knowing where I was. I woke up again later to the distant sound of a radio and ran to throw up in the bathtub.

Not long after that, the concierge waved me over. "A few people have been inquiring about when you might sell," he said.

"Who says I'm selling?" I asked.

"It's not a rental unit," he said.

"I'm not renting it to anyone."

"The board doesn't allow units to sit empty."

"I'm paying the fees."

"It's just that you can't hold a unit for investment purposes."

I burst into tears.

A woman in her early seventies walked into the lobby just then, an ancient cocker spaniel with gummy eyes snuffling behind her. "Vlad," she snapped at the concierge. "What has this thug said to upset you, huh?" she asked me.

I was a mess by this point, spluttering out some kind of explanation, wiping my nose on my sleeve.

"Ah," she said, a hedge of eyebrow rising above her glasses, "so you're the daughter?"

I nodded at the woman with the dog. "Forgive me," the woman said, lowering her eyebrows and patting my forearm. "*HaMakom yenachem et'chem b'toch shar avay'lay Tzion vee'Yerushalayim.*"

—

I put the file into my briefcase and take a cab home at the end of the day, the prospect of leaving the evidence of someone's trauma on a bus just too sad. As I climb the fire escape at the back of my building a train shudders by on the elevated track twenty feet behind me. I need to move, I say to myself, as I say to myself almost every day. I'm not supposed to be almost forty, single, and living in a shitty apartment. It was a temporary move, a way of extricating myself quickly from Michael, but I've been here now for nearly two years.

I met Michael six years ago, in AA. I started going to meetings after losing my first job—not immediately, but after the night I woke up in the field of my old high school, face-down on the track, no memory of how I'd ended up there, unable to find my shoes or my bra. I'd certainly been going to meetings long enough to know that dating anyone in the group was against all the rules.

Three months in, though, about the time Michael and I first talked about having sex, we decided we were fine to share a bottle of wine over dinner. Just one. And only with dinner. I can tell you that every single glass he poured, I measured against mine. If we were going to share a bottle, I was going to have my half. If he went to the bathroom, I quickly topped up my glass. I started stopping at a bar after work to get some vodka into my system before I got home. Before long, we were gulping down wine, in competition, and of course a bottle lasted only twenty minutes and what were we going to do then? It was only seven p.m.; why, the wine shop on the corner was still open, better get the two-litre jug this time, you know, just thinking ahead, saving you a trip tomorrow. But there's never a tomorrow when you're drinking to go black. I had to stop before the light went out for good.

I plant myself on the couch and pull Robin's file out of my briefcase. The first picture I come across was taken on May 16th. Just her face: grey eyes looking away from the camera, chin jutting out. Her hair is an indeterminate brown halo. Her skin is so pale it is almost translucent, like egg white.

The initial medical report identifies rickets as the likely cause of the bowing of her lower legs. She's being treated for vitamin D deficiency, giardiasis, pinworm and anemia. The rest of the report reads like an autopsy. No semen in her vagina. No saliva other than her own. A list of fibres found on her body including bark, hay and bird feathers and a note about traces of raccoon feces found in her hair.

Her hearing is normal and she has suffered no damage to her vocal cords. The police had played a recording of a woman's voice speaking in a dozen different languages but she showed no signs of comprehension. The report concludes that from a medical standpoint, her mutism may be a consequence of head injury, brain damage, or cognitive disability, or related to autism or a learning or sensory processing disorder.

Jacqui takes an entirely different approach. In her notes, she writes that while some children stop speaking entirely in response to a traumatic incident, in most cases, mutism is selective and related to a high degree of social anxiety. A child might speak quite confidently at home but remain silent at school, for instance. If that is the case, Robin may well speak in an environment where she is comfortable.

Melanie, the social worker who has been working with Robin for the past three months, doesn't appear to have put Robin at ease. She had started with a number of standard play-based aptitude tests—shape and pattern recognition, logic puzzles, counting. Apparently Robin had whacked the various plastic primary-coloured shapes into their corresponding holes then hurled the whole box at a wall. Good for you, I think. I'd be insulted as well.

But that wasn't Melanie's assessment. *Erratic expressions of anger*, she wrote in Robin's file, followed by *oppositional disorder?* in brackets, implying Robin was refusing rather than unable to speak. On the basis of Melanie's assessment, Robin has been offered a place in a Section 23 school, for kids unable to participate in a regular classroom, but they don't have room for her until January. In an ideal world, we'd help her find some way to communicate before that, which gives us just over four months. Thus far she has remained silent with everyone involved in her care.

In a photo taken this summer, Robin's hair is brushed and trimmed and pulled back in a ponytail. She is wearing a white shirt. She gazes away from the camera, same grey eyes and translucent skin, her chin softer this time, but the overall effect still haunting.

I put down the file and walk to the front window to pull the curtains closed. It has started to rain; smokers huddle under the awning of the bar across the street. If they were to look up they'd see me in outline, a black shape at a third-storey window, a woman without a face.

There is a photo among my mother's things, one I wish she'd never kept, of the girl they adopted in 1975. The defiance in the girl's face is painful—a futile attempt to deny her vulnerability. She is only three years old; whatever memories she had then would be lost, at least consciously, to later experiences. It would be the unconscious that would haunt her.

Hazel and Victor, who had both lost their parents to the Holocaust, were in their late thirties when they adopted me. The rabbi at their synagogue had approached them. My mother, a young Romanian Jewish refugee known to the Rabbi, had died. It was only at the end of his life that Victor was willing to share some of the more difficult aspects of my mother's story. She had apparently arrived in Canada as a pregnant teen. There was no indication of who my father might have been. Two years after I was born she had taken her own life.

I likely hadn't formed a secure attachment in those first years with my biological mother, a teenager on her own in a foreign country who didn't want a baby—didn't want a baby so much that she didn't even want her own life. I am reminded of a video we watched in my first-year psych class. Those rhesus monkeys who'd been separated from their mothers—even when they were reintroduced to a social group they had remained withdrawn, despondent. They would always be disconnected, feel unsafe in some very fundamental way.

I have seen this in other children. I have felt it in them. I recognized it in Izzie the first time I met her. It was my very first year on the job and I told myself: Whatever the feelings this evokes in you, this is what you signed up for. You have the tools and the training to do this.

The goal was to provide Izzie and her father with the support and communication skills needed to develop and maintain a relationship. Chris was new to her life—when her mother had a near-fatal overdose, rather than letting his daughter go into care, he'd stepped up. Chris had been granted custody and Lori was in long-term rehab. With Chris's consent, I had called Lori to introduce myself. There was the likelihood that I would be asked to help her and Izzie in the rebuilding of their relationship once, and if, she successfully completed her program.

When I met her, Izzie was an anxious six-year-old who would only go to sleep in Chris's truck. We got her to try sleeping in the apartment on weeknights, and she'd been managing to do this more nights than not, when she suddenly started refusing to get out of the truck to go to school in the mornings.

I suggested Chris talk to her teacher, the principal, try and find out whether something had happened, whether she was being bullied at school. I knew that Izzie didn't have any friends and that Chris took her straight to her classroom in the mornings rather than letting her play in the schoolyard. I'd been encouraging him to talk to other parents, try and cultivate some sense of community that could lead to friendships and play dates in the future, work to normalize things for his daughter socially as much as he could.

But he couldn't get Izzie out of the truck that week. And he couldn't leave her in the truck so that he could go into the school to talk to her teacher. He'd had to take her to work with him. After three days of this, both he and his boss were losing patience.

So I offered to try.

While this was technically beyond the boundaries of my job, I met them outside Izzie's school at 8:30 the following Monday morning. I opened the door of Chris's Chevy and slid into the cab beside Izzie, who was still wearing her pyjamas.

"Had breakfast?" I asked.

"Cheerios," she said, pointing to a mug on the dashboard.

"Will you be okay here with me while your dad goes in to talk to your teacher?" I asked.

She nodded and Chris sighed. "See you in a bit, kiddo," he said.

"Something happen at school?" I asked, as we watched Chris walk through the front door of the school.

"No," she said.

"Why don't you want to go?"

"Recess."

"You don't like recess? Is someone being mean to you?"

"I saw her."

"You saw who?"

"Her."

"You mean your mom? You saw your mom at recess?"

"Outside the fence."

"Did she talk to you?"

"No."

"How did it make you feel?"

"I don't know," she said, starting to cry. "Dad will be mad."

"He won't be mad at you, Izzie."

"She'll be mad."

"You haven't done anything wrong, sweetheart. She isn't supposed to be here. She's supposed to be in her program, right? She's still got a few more months."

Izzie had her chin to her chest.

"You know what I used to love?" I said. "Indoor recess. You know, like when it's raining."

"Yeah," she said, lifting her head. "We do crafts."

"What if we suggest indoor recess for the next little while?"

She seemed to think that was a good idea. "Maybe we should get inside before the bell goes so we have a chance to talk to your teacher."

"But I'm in my PJs," she said.

"I'm sure your dad put some clothes in your backpack." I reached for her bag on the floor and placed it on her lap.

She unzipped her backpack and out came jeans, a pink sweatshirt and a soft lunch box adorned with a sparkly Ariel.

She held on to my forearm with both of her hands as we walked into the school that day. After she'd changed in the girls' bathroom and I'd talked to her teacher, she turned to me and said: "Can you come tomorrow?"

I did have a moment of hesitation, but just a moment.

Without words, it's going to take some creative ways of finding clues to who Robin is, what she has been through, where she belongs. That part doesn't worry me; what does is that Robin's photos evoke a feeling of recognition. It's as if I am looking at the ghost who lives in me.

—

I buy muffins on my way in to work. In the consulting room I tape a large sheet of paper across the table and place a box of pencil crayons on top. My head is cracking from last night's wine, but at times like this, facing a daunting challenge, I almost like the rawness of being compromised by a hangover: my defences fall away.

When Robin's case manager drops her off for her first of what will be two forty-five minute sessions a week with me, Jacqui ushers her in. She stands behind the girl, holding her by the shoulders. Robin's eyes wander everywhere around the room, taking in everything except my face with its forced smile. She is smaller than I'd imagined, her head looking too big for her body, but I know from her file that she's put on twelve pounds since being placed in emergency foster care. I wouldn't put her at eleven if it weren't for her face; she has lost some of the skim-milk pallor of the first photograph and has developed a certain definition around her cheekbones and her eyes.

"Robin, this is Lila. She is the person I explained would be taking over from Melanie. I'll leave you two to get acquainted, okay?" She squeezes the girl's shoulders before leaving. From the way Robin turns her head toward Jacqui's voice, I can see she feels some comfort with her. She might not make eye contact, but she is responsive. Jacqui's loving and gently authoritative way has that effect on most people. She should have been a parent; she is often mine.

I point at the chair opposite me at the table. Robin sits down, never looking at me. My chair is slightly lower: I want us at the same eye level. "Do you want to take off your coat?" I ask quietly, miming shrugging off my own. She shakes her head. I lift the box of muffins from the filing cabinet and set it on the table. I open the lid. She leans over and stares into the box. "Have one," I say, nodding my head. She pauses, chewing her bottom lip. "Well, I'm having at least one," I say.

Robin reaches in, her hand covered in scratches as if she's been picking raspberries, and quickly plucks a muffin from the box. She cups it in her hand holding it against her chest, then she bends her head and starts pecking at the muffin. I can see why Jacqui called her Robin.

I ask whether she wants another one. She snatches one from the box and shoves it into her coat pocket. She takes another and thrusts it into her other pocket. She clearly grasps the essence of whatever I'm saying. "I'm glad you like them," I say.

I point at the paper and pencil crayons. It's best to start with something tangible between us. "I thought we could do some drawing this morning." I take a dark blue pencil crayon from the box and start to draw a rudimentary picture of a house. "When I was your age, I lived in a house with my mother and father." I draw three stick figures beside our little Victorian row house.

Robin leans in to study the picture. I offer her the box of pencil crayons but she quickly sits back in her chair and crosses her arms across her chest.

"It wasn't a big house, but I had my own bedroom," I say, indicating one of the windows on the second floor. "And we had a backyard with an apple tree." I draw our rectangular yard and a gnarly tree. "The apples weren't good to eat; crab apples, tough sour little things that shouldn't really be called apples at all."

"And my school," I say, drawing a dotted line, "was a couple of blocks away." I draw a long rectangle punctuated with windows. "I loved school, at least I did until math started to get confusing. And on Thursday afternoons, I walked here," adding another dotted line, "for my piano lesson with Mrs. Nagata."

Robin slowly unfolds her arms and places her fingertips on the edge of the table. She starts moving her fingers against the laminate. I place my own fingertips on the edge of the table. "She made me practice my scales over and over," I say, moving my fingers in succession. "Sometimes she made me practice with my eyes closed." Robin's eyelids flutter closed as mine do.

"It was only after a year of playing nothing but scales that Mrs. Nagata finally let me start on a piece of music. Minuet in D Minor. Pretty standard." I start to hum the first few bars of the minuet.

I watch Robin for some time, not wanting to interrupt as her fingers move up and down an imaginary keyboard. And then she stops, drops her hands into her lap and opens her eyes blankly to the ceiling.

Learning to play the piano was one of those things on a long list of things that my mother had never had the opportunity to do, and so it had fallen to me. I inherited it not as opportunity but as responsibility. I was faithful to my lessons, diligent about practicing, at least until adolescence. It wasn't just a case of rebellion; I had started listening to recordings of

Glenn Gould and Keith Jarrett and I found myself more interested in the sounds beneath the notes—the humming and the grunts, the tiny explosions of breath—which seemed to be telling a more difficult story. My relationship to music was a technical one, not an emotional one. They were musicians, I was not.

But this broken bird of a girl might be. Nothing in her hand positioning suggests she's ever had lessons. The music is just there in her, as if awaiting permission.

I have my father's radio in a corner of my office, a clunky old thing with a teak veneer. He gave it to me a few years ago when I complained that it was impossible to find a simple radio anymore. I heave the thing over to the table and turn it on. Robin is fascinated by it. She twists the tuner very quickly at first, before discovering that the slower you turn it, the more precisely you land. She homes in on a piece of classical music. She wiggles the tuner until the tone is clear. It's a string piece, vaguely familiar, neither fast nor slow: an andante or moderato.

Robin places her fingertips on top of the radio and begins to play along. The piece ends and gives way to an ad for car insurance. Robin smacks the radio hard.

"Robin," I say, placing my hand on top of hers. "Be gentle, okay? This was my father's, I'm quite attached to it."

She stares at my hand with some confusion.

"My father," I repeat.

I point to the tallest of the stick figures in my drawing. "My father." She points to the other two. "Me, and my mother," I say. "And our house."

She puts her finger to the page as if to draw with it. I grab a pencil crayon and put it into her hand. She holds it in an unusual way, between her middle and forefinger. She stabs the paper and draws a hard line, tearing the paper.

"It's not very good paper," I say, "go a little easier on it. Here, can I show you?" I reposition the pencil between her thumb and forefinger. She draws four unsteady lines: a rectangle. "Is this *your* house?" I ask.

She draws a tiny stick figure in one corner of the rectangle. She points to herself, punching her sternum with her finger, then sits back in her chair, pleased.

My interpretations are always more literal than Jacqui's. In this way our work is complementary. In our debriefing session, I tell Jacqui that I think Robin's drawing was an attempt to convey something of the domestic world she left—one where she was shut in a room alone or imprisoned in some way. Jacqui sees it in metaphorical terms—Robin imprisoned by her lack of language, isolated from others in this way; trapped by the inability to communicate something of her internal world. Neither of us thinks these two interpretations need be mutually exclusive.

I smile at the thought of Robin patting the radio as she was leaving this morning, as if to apologize for smacking it.

"What is it?" Jacqui asks.

"She has music in her head."

—

I am back at my mother's condo on Saturday morning to deal with the contents of her storage locker. Boxes full of linens and crystal that my mother had never even opened. A lot of old books. There's nothing here to feel particularly sentimental about. I might feel a little more emotional about her things if I had children and was thinking of saving something to pass on. I find myself retrieving a collection of marble eggs from a box marked for donation to B'nai Brith. I pack them carefully into an old shoe box that I will shove to the back of my closet at home.

Having set aside the boxes for donation, I take the elevator up to the fifth floor. Since my mother died in July, I've grown much more familiar with this place. I even take comfort in the light in my mother's apartment, its southern view all the way down to the CN Tower; beyond it, horizon. I hadn't seen the horizon growing up downtown. My parents had remained in our modest, crumbling Victorian house at College and Spadina long past the time when Jewish neighbours and businesses had left the area and migrated north. I'd always assumed staying put had suited them both, and imagined my mother living out her days on Major Street, continuing to pull a bundle buggy into Kensington Market well into her nineties. My mother's sudden declaration that she was moving to a condo at Bathurst and Sheppard had really thrown me, even if it didn't exactly come out of nowhere.

Elena, an old friend of my mother's from the neighbour-hood, had moved to an apartment at Bathurst and Lawrence after her husband died. On Wednesday nights for several years my mother had taken a twenty-five-minute bus ride up Bathurst to spend the evening playing mah-jong at Elena's apartment. Shortly before my father died, Elena had told Hazel that her kids had bought her a condo at Bathurst and Sheppard— new building, concierge, fancy. As soon as my father died, my mother was on the phone to a real estate agent and I realized I knew even less than I thought about a woman I had never known well. In Victor's absence there was somewhere else she needed to go. A new neighbourhood, a new synagogue. A place both new and somewhere back in time. Somewhere she couldn't take me.

Her impeccable English began to falter as soon as she moved north. She began to forget certain words, stammering the equivalent in Ukrainian, a language she'd always claimed to have forgotten—"I left so young," she would always say; "English taught me how to see the world." And sometimes: "Ukrainian taught me the words for ugly things."

I hadn't recognized the signs of her dementia. My mother had moved into this new condo, proud to be the unit's first inhabitant, but left most of her boxes unpacked. She'd never really inhabited it at all. It could certainly use some cheering up now. A brighter coat of paint and a more colourful carpet would help. And maybe some new kitchen cupboards. I have a fleeting moment of wondering if I could ever live here. It would be such a different life, away from the bars and the streetcar tracks and the train. Shopping in strip malls and plazas, kosher stores. And where is the nearest liquor store? Nowhere that I can walk to. Perhaps the question is less could I live here than should I. There would even be room enough for a grand piano, I think. Hah. That would show Vlad.

—

Robin is sitting in the waiting room on Tuesday morning with Mirabelle, her case manager. She looks like a typical kid in her Roots hoodie and Gap jeans. Look more closely, though, and you can see the raised scars on the backs of her hands, her wrists thickened by rickets, her legs so bowed that her knees cannot touch despite the rigidity of her posture, her clenched jaw.

I wave at her, trying to draw focus from those opaque eyes, and she rises, expressionless, without so much as a nod to Mirabelle, and follows me into my office. She heads straight for the radio, a girl on a mission, and stares at it, willing it to make sound.

I walk over to the filing cabinet and show her that by twisting the volume dial to the right she can bring the radio to life. She turns the knob and frowns at the voice of the newsreader. I tap the other dial. "You can change the station."

She is much gentler with the radio than last time, slowly cycling through static, listening in, and eventually finding a classical station, one playing something at least two hundred years old. Satisfied, she joins me at the table.

I slide the drawing we were working on last time into the space between us. "Do you remember I showed you where my bedroom was?" I point to a window on the second floor. "It was painted a light blue like this," I say, drawing a square which I begin to shade in. "I never did go through a pink stage."

I continue to narrate as I draw. "My bed was up against this wall, with a little night table beside it where I kept my books. I had a checkered bedspread and I slept with this stuffed duck every night. Quackers. And on the opposite wall . . . there was a dresser where I kept my clothes and a closet for the, you know, fancier things. I had this old rocking horse—I'm not sure I can draw a rocking horse, but maybe this will give you an idea."

Robin follows my lines with her eyes then traces the outline of my poor approximation of a horse with her finger. She touches the bedspread and the duck.

"I was wondering whether you might want to add any details to your picture," I say, tapping her drawing with the end of my pencil.

She stares at her drawing and slowly picks out a brown pencil crayon. She draws a small rectangle against one wall.

"Is this where you sleep?" I ask, leaning my head to the side and closing my eyes. She leans her own head to the side, in confirmation possibly, or perhaps just copying my movements.

"What about a window?" I ask, adding one inside my square.

Robin picks up a black pencil crayon and draws another rectangle in the top right corner.

"I could see the leaves of a tree outside my window," I say, drawing a tree branch sprouting oak leaves. "What did you see out your window?" I ask, pointing to hers.

She draws one black foot, then another. The view from a basement window.

I point at my duck, then my rocking horse. "Did you have any toys?"

In the upper left-hand corner she carefully draws a spider's web. And in the lower left-hand corner, a spider. She taps the spider and moves her fingers to show the spider climbing up the wall above her bed.

"Your friend," I say, patting the spider too.

She pushes her chair back from the table and walks over to the filing cabinet. She pats the radio much like she did the spider. Her picture might have looked barren initially, but she is revealing evidence of life within it and there is music somewhere in this world.

"Where is the door to your room?" I ask, pointing at the door of my office.

She shakes her head and I'm not sure if she has understood me. I show her the closet door in my picture and add the door to my room, which opened onto the landing of the second floor.

She shakes her head more vehemently.

No door? Or perhaps no door she was allowed to open.

What about a bathroom? I wonder. But drawing a toilet is beyond me. I draw the universal symbol of a girl in an A-line skirt, but Robin only frowns.

"Come," I say, reaching out my hand. I open the door and take her down the hall to the bathroom. I point at the symbol on the door.

"Uh," she utters in recognition.

Back in my office, she adds a picture of a girl in an A-line skirt in the corner of the room. But she isn't done: she draws a large cross on the wall over the bed. And on the adjacent wall, a circle with spokes curved like waves. A flower? The sun? A pinwheel? I hold her picture at arm's-length, trying to make sense of this unusual trinity of symbols. I could take her to church and I can take her to the bathroom, but I wouldn't know where to find her flower-sun-wheel.

At the end of the day, I sit on one of the white plastic chairs in the waiting room and look through the pile of old magazines, searching for images. I tear out pictures of things people are commonly afraid of—fire, water, insects, buildings, crowds, airplanes, black cats—as well as more benign images of things like flowers, an Easter rabbit, donuts, puppies, the sun. I cut and glue these images onto cardstock in preparation for our next appointment. It's a simple way to begin identifying what she has been exposed to, where some of her fears might lie, where she might find comfort. I can get more and more specific with imagery over time, narrow it down, isolate the details. Is it all water you are afraid of or just dark murky lakes?

Robin goes straight to the radio again at the beginning of our next appointment. I haven't changed the station in her absence and she looks pleased when she turns it on. I have her sit down beside me at the table, and introduce the images as if we are about to play a game of cards.

"Two piles," I say, "one for happy things, things you love, and one for things that you don't like." I show her the image of puppies, clasp it to my chest and smile. "This one definitely makes me happy," I say, laying it down.

She likes the puppies too. She likes all the animals and the insects. The only other image she picks up is of a woman at a piano. She puts her fingers onto the tiny keyboard and very quietly hums. She does this for several minutes, then pauses before resuming, as if beginning a second movement.

At the end of the hour she tucks the image of the piano into her pocket and looks at me sheepishly.

"It's fine," I assure her.

When I walk home that night, I take a long and meandering route through the university campus. I'm curious to know whether the grand piano I used to like to play as an undergraduate is still standing in the corner of West Hall. The high ceilings and wooden floor had allowed the sound to mushroom in the space, and although the acoustics amplified my mistakes, it was hard not to sound good when I was playing well.

I can hear Tchaikovsky as soon as I enter the college, a waterfall of notes flooding the halls. I sit down on a worn stair, lean my back into the wall and close my eyes. Playing piano here offered me some rare respite years ago. My mother had pushed me into sciences, pre-med, and while I remained diligent and studious I'd felt such weight pressing down, as if I were being squeezed between earth and sky. In the months before I wrote my MCAT, I worked with a strange and slightly smelly gnome of a math tutor in the atrium of Robarts Library every weekday evening. As soon as he left I would take the elevator to the eleventh floor, crawl under a desk and sleep into the next day.

My mother had insisted I go to the doctor after another night of failing to come home, said I must have a virus of some sort, she was sure of it. The doctor referred me to a counsellor, a social worker who didn't get anywhere near the deeper issues but did help me reach the decision not to apply to medical school that year. This devastated my mother, sending her into a prolonged depression.

The unknown pianist has finished the Tchaikovsky piece and I suddenly stand up, self-conscious about having been sitting there listening. I push my way out of the building through a side exit and skirt around the northern field, where soccer games are at various stages of play. Crossing the street, I wander up Philosopher's Walk, past the Faculty of Music, toward the Royal Conservatory. A window at the back of the conservatory is open, a soprano sending notes out into the evening.

I decide to pop into the conservatory bookstore, thinking I might look for a collection of simplified versions of classic piano pieces like one I had as a child. I take my time selecting a couple of beginner volumes then find myself drifting over to the piano concertos, wondering if I might start practicing again myself. My father had started my musical education by exposing me to the works of many of the major Russian and eastern European composers. He later directed me to other, more obscure composers, men I would only later realize had been Romanian Jews. It was his quiet way, I suppose, of trying to connect me to a lost history.

—

I've changed our twice-weekly appointments to a double session on Wednesdays, giving us more time for what I have in mind. Although I have Jacqui's go-ahead, I still wait to hear the outer door close after Mirabelle drops Robin off before I reach for both of our jackets. Robin stares at her coat, uncomprehending. I sit down beside her and pull a collection of easy piano pieces from my bag. I place the fingers of my right hand on the keyboard printed on the cover and start to play Bach's Minuet in D Minor. When I start humming along, Robin's mouth cracks open into something like a smile, revealing her small grey teeth.

Her hand crawls across the table until she reaches the edge of the book's cover. "Try it," I say, nodding. Once her fingers are on the keys, I lift her elbow, straighten out her wrist, and start to hum the minuet again. This time it is unambiguous: she is smiling.

I push back my chair and stand up, putting my jacket on. "We're going to play a real piano."

On the bus, she sits beside me, her face turned toward the window. She watches people, staring as if she can't be seen. I imagine her watching people's feet passing by her basement window. When we reach the college, she seems a bit intimidated by its grandeur. She tiptoes up the wooden staircase, wincing whenever the floor creaks. Classes are underway. A few students linger in the hallway and Robin keeps her eyes to the floor. At the distinctive clacking of administrative heels, she steps behind me, burying her face in my back. When we get to West Hall, she stares up at the vaulted wooden ceiling. Rectangles of colour fall across the wooden floor as the sun pours through the stained glass windows. Robin drifts around the room with her arms outstretched, dipping her toes in and out of blue and red blocks of light.

I make my way over to the Steinway in the far corner, pull out the bench and sit down. I play a few simple chords and pat the space to my left without turning around. Soon I can feel Robin's presence behind me, peering over my shoulder, studying my hands, and then she is at my side, placing her own fingers on the keys, tentatively playing a D with her index finger. She inhales sharply at the sound and looks up to the ceiling as if to follow it. I play a D major chord and then reach for Robin's hand. She lets me position her fingers with mine overtop and together we press down on the keys. Robin's face transforms into a collage of confusion, hesitation, wonder. She pulls her hands away and stares at the keyboard, as if needing to replay the steps in her mind in order to absorb what has just happened.

I start to play Pachelbel's Canon, perhaps the most famous piece in D major. It's only when Robin exhales at the end of the second variation that I realize she's been holding her breath. I try inhaling when she does, hold my breath along with hers, defer to her instinctive sense of phrasing, so natural it is as if she has written the music herself.

And then I suddenly realize the time. "We have to go," I say, quickly standing up. Robin pulls back, a bit startled. "Sorry," I say, tapping my watch, "Mirabelle."

On my way home that night, I think about how Robin's musical gift could anchor her in the right circumstances, something she could always rely on, whatever the state of her world, whoever its people. I wonder if I could arrange for piano lessons, find the right teacher. I know that I am stretching the boundaries, but I'm just thinking.

Izzie had asked me to accompany her into school every day. Despite knowing how doing so would be perceived professionally, I did it anyway. What mattered was that she felt safe. So I waited outside her school every morning for two weeks in order to walk her into the building and up to her classroom. And I accepted Chris's offers of rides to work.

At the end of the second week, Chris had stopped his truck outside my office and reached over and squeezed my thigh. "We make a good team," he'd said.

I let his hand rest there. I took in his large knuckles, the sparse black hairs between his finger joints, the fact that he chewed his nails. It wasn't that I was attracted to him, but I spent the weekend fantasizing about what it might be like to be part of their world. Helping Izzie with her homework at a round kitchen table. Chris returning home from work and cracking a beer, kissing us both on the head before making a pot of his infamous chili. Running through the sprinkler in the backyard with Izzie on hot afternoons while Chris finished building his daughter a treehouse.

Then, just as Chris was pulling up outside the school on Monday morning, Lori suddenly appeared like a bear out of the woods, smelling danger. She was shaking with rage, but she had enough sense not to scream in front of her daughter. She mouthed the words "Get the fuck away from us," at me. And while I would report her for being in violation of a court agreement, she would report me for ethical breaches that would cost me my job and almost completely derail my career.

I get off the streetcar two stops early tonight. I don't even mask my intent, plunking a two-litre bottle of Pinot Grigio onto the counter at the wine store.

—

Robin has memorized the minuet by the third time we sit down at the piano. It must have taken me six months or more to get this far with Mrs. Nagata. Last week we worked on the phrasing and acoustics of the piece, but today, I think we'll push the music aside and see what we can create without any notes in front of us.

I start with an A minor chord in order to establish a mood. Then I play the notes one at a time, nodding at her to do the same. She seems unsatisfied playing in the lower octave, and comes round to my right-hand side to play the notes two octaves higher. I try a sequence of tonic triads, which Robin repeats, adding three more. So we're playing a game. Her six chords, my nine, then her twelve. But I stumble at twelve, and have to start again, which delights her. She laughs, but quickly covers her mouth, embarrassed by the sound that has escaped. I break into a smile, astonished. I feel my eyes well up: her voice is in the room, an echo.

"Robin," I say, beaming.

She moves her hand away from her mouth and reveals a crooked and vulnerable grey grin.

She doesn't linger with me in that moment, though, but quickly reaches for the Liszt piano concerto. I've started working on the first movement, an allegro maestoso. The last third of the movement has a difficult descent of chromatic octaves. I love its drama, but I'm not sure I will ever be able to play it.

Robin follows along with the music, even turning the pages today. As I approach the descending octaves, she inhales as deeply as I do. If I slow it right down to an andante, I might just about manage to get through it. I can sense Robin nodding her head as I plod through it at a fraction of its speed.

Afterwards, waiting at the bus stop for too long in the cold, I suggest walking for a bit. We make our way along Harbord Street, past the bakery my mother used to dismiss as overpriced, and then I cup Robin's elbow and lead her back through the bakery door, into the expensive humidity of the place.

I hand Robin some tongs and tell her to pick anything she likes from the bins of cookies in front of us. She picks a rather austere looking gingersnap. I opt for a sugar cookie covered in coloured sprinkles just in case hers is disappointing, and order myself a cup of coffee. Robin leans in and inhales my coffee.

"Does it remind you of somewhere?" I ask. "Of home?"

She furrows her brow in some expression of worry or uncertainty.

I break my cookie in two once we are outside again and offer her half. She does the same with hers.

We stop outside a bookstore and look at the display in the window. She points at a book with a cover illustration of a girl against a mountain backdrop—an illustrated edition of *Heidi*. I open the door to the shop and reach into the window well in order to pass her the book. She glows at the sight of it now materialized in her hands and delicately turns the first couple of pages. I watch her as she studies the illustrations and wonder what in particular drew her to it, what she is seeing in the story of the girl whose mother has died and whose aunt pawns her off on a gruff old Grandpa in the mountains who has no appetite for children.

Starting to feel we've hijacked the display copy for long enough, I gently take the book from her and place it on the counter. The woman behind the register breaks the silence, asking, "Do you need a bag?"

Robin reaches for the book on the counter and clasps it against her chest.

She now carries that book with her, always. She tucks it inside her coat. Whenever we're at the piano, she places it partially open on top, positioning it just as she saw it displayed in the bookstore window.

Today, I can feel Robin's body tensing beside mine as the descent of octaves approaches. I'm finally ready to embark on it with greater speed. One page into the passage I can hear her grinding her teeth. I keep on, tearing through it, as if together we are running from madmen chasing us down a mountain, and once we are in the clear, on level ground, Robin claps and shouts a raspy "Ah!"

She shouts. The girl who doesn't speak has just shouted, and that one syllable is so full of life it's like the first cry of a newborn. I pull Robin into me, hugging her at this awkward angle as we sit side by side on the bench. I kiss the top of her head and start to cry.

Jacqui would want me to examine Robin's vocalization and my reaction to it in exacting detail. She would consider it my professional obligation to do so. But when I'm writing up my notes later in the afternoon, I make the decision to omit any reference to it. Robin and I are in the very fragile stages of building a shared reality. It is a tender thing, a sprout to nurture, and I don't want to risk the intrusion of a more objective analysis, which Robin might experience as distancing.

At our weekly review meeting Jacqui tells me we are going to need to offer something tangible, some concrete indication of progress to Children's Aid very soon.

I appeal to her for more time. This is an exceptional case. Building trust and establishing communication in the absence of language requires both more time and more creative means. I am hopeful, I tell Jacqui, that we are really on the edge of finding some common understanding. This is not just about figuring out Robin's identity, where she came from, who might be accountable, but about helping her find her voice. Chances are she's not going back to where she comes from. What she needs are tools to take with her wherever she goes next. I am hopeful that something can be healed.

Robin awakens an optimism in me that I want to harness. I stop at the hardware store on my way home to pick out paint chips. Then I stop at the wine store for some boxes for my books. One of the staff members is mopping up the contents of a bottle of Jameson's that has crashed to the floor and the smell of alcohol floods me, the craving still as deep and dangerous.

I will get free of this place, all the associations, the bad matches, the bars, the thunder of the train and its lonely cry at night, the obliteration of senses, the lack of horizon, the lost sun. I grab four boxes and get out of there as quickly as I can.

—

It's taken most of a day to paint my mother's living and dining room. The butter-cream yellow I've chosen has softened the glare of the walls against the harsh winter light. I've been listening to old tapes of my father's while I paint. I found a box of them along with an old tape recorder in my mother's storage locker this morning. Among the classical music, composers he'd introduced me to, there was a boxed collection of folk songs from the Danube. The cover is a clichéd and faded photograph of a river, women in long white skirts with garlands of flowers in their hair waving from a grassy shore. The music is a little accordion-heavy for my taste, but the songs are lively; they do at least keep my paint roller moving at a good pace.

I'm leaving the apartment to go and grab a sandwich at the end of the day when I run into the old lady with the dog on the elevator. "You're painting," she says, evidence of this freckling my sweatshirt, my face, my hair. "You don't have a man who can do that for you?"

"I enjoy it," I say. "It's kind of meditative."

"My granddaughter is a feminist," she says, with some distaste.

I turn to the dog, who is digging his snout into something in a corner. I'm not sure he can see at all through the cataracts and the gunk in his eyes.

"There's a lady on the seventh floor who always rests her groceries in this corner and he never forgets this," she says. "I think it's the fish."

I hold the elevator door open once we reach the ground floor while the dog finishes his investigation.

"Leonard," the woman says, tugging at his lead, trying to coax him out into the hall.

I follow their six-footed shuffle down the hall toward the lobby. A baby wails behind the door of 102; a stroller is propped up beside the door. Leonard stops to sniff it.

"You should come to the board meeting next week," the woman says over her shoulder. "It's never dull. And it's my turn to make the sandwiches."

"I was just wondering," I stammer, "do you know anything about the local schools?"

"You having a baby?" she says, turning around.

I don't know how to reply; I just wish she didn't look so incredulous.

"Might need to find a man first," she says, laughing.

"It's not like that," I say.

Her mouth opens. "Oh," she says, nodding, "that explains things."

"It's not whatever you're thinking."

"None of my business," she says, waving her hand. "Anyway, you should talk to Leona. She's the girl who takes the minutes. She's got three little ones, she'll be able to tell you what's what."

There's a small strip mall at the corner of Bathurst and Sheppard where I get myself a falafel and some rice pudding. I crunch back to my mother's building over the icy sidewalks in the dusk. The building rises like a tiered cake out of the ground, surrounded by modest bungalows on all sides.

There is comfort in entering the building to the combined smells of various dinners being baked, fried and roasted at this hour.

I eat my sandwich in the dark on the floor of the solarium, watching the city's transformation into night. I can imagine sitting here with Robin and counting the lights as they appear, popping up like flowers in spring, making a game of it: the lights below and the stars above.

———

Jacqui and I have a meeting scheduled with Mirabelle and her supervisor tomorrow morning. Apparently they want to talk about the possibility of moving Robin out of emergency foster care and into a group home.

I've felt nauseous about this all morning and while I'm trying not to communicate my anxiety to Robin, she senses it: I am failing with the allegro, nowhere up to speed.

How could moving her into a group home possibly benefit her? She's too young. Move her now, place her among a bunch of seriously troubled kids and she will be stamped with every damning label in the book. She will be bounced from a series of homes for being developmentally delayed, hoarding food, lacking social skills, she will be provoked and antagonized, throw things, run away or set fire to the curtains and eventually, when she turns eighteen, she will be turned over to the street. She will go unrecognized and unknown.

Robin moves the score closer to her side of the bench and turns back to the first page. She places her fingers on the keys. She's going to play this? And to my absolute astonishment she begins, playing at precisely the right tempo. She continues beyond the first page. It appears she isn't reading the music but playing from memory. With both hands. She plays the first three pages, stopping where the tempo slows right down, and lowers her hands to her lap.

We sit side by side, still, on the bench. Eventually I tap my watch, not wanting to break the spell that encloses us. We make our way out of the hall, down the worn steps, away from the building and toward the bus stop in reverential silence.

I watch Robin stride up the steps onto the bus and drop our tickets into the collection box. She's not the wild mouse I first encountered. She leads us to a seat on the right side of the aisle and sits by the window, which offers her the best view of pedestrians on the sidewalk. She likes to watch people when they are not aware of being watched and she presses her fingertip to the glass every time she sees a dog out the window.

At Spadina Avenue two large women board the bus, shuffling down the aisle with their buggies full of groceries. They take a seat immediately behind us, talking animatedly in some eastern European language. Robin whisks her head around at the sound and stares at them directly, making eye contact in a way I have never seen her do before. She clearly understands, but she still doesn't speak.

"You like the gossip of old ladies?" one of them says to her in English.

Robin continues to stare.

"Excuse me," I say, "but what language were you speaking?"

"Georgian," says the larger of the two women.

I turn back around to face the front of the bus, leaning back into my seat, this information settling in uncomfortably. I can feel my diaphragm catch light. This is a critical piece of information, one I am legally and professionally bound to share. It's a piece of the puzzle that will get us much closer to knowing who Robin is and where she comes from. It is good information; it just doesn't feel good to me.

Perhaps Robin understands this, because rather than offering them anything in reply, she takes my hand and leans her head on my shoulder. She is making a choice in this moment. And I am going to follow her lead.

ADAM

ADAM AWAKES to a splash of warm rain. His tongue leaves his mouth of its own accord, bringing relief as water tumbles over his forehead, down his nose and onto his lips. It tastes overly sweet, like the juice of a bruised nectarine. He leans his head back, closes his eyes and lets his jaw go slack. His temples spasm with each heartbeat and he feels a nail of pain being driven between his eyes.

A torrent of laughter falls from above, and he cranes his head to look up, squinting into the light. Faces in shadow surround a circle, the sky beyond them a wash of Navajo blue. Someone is pissing down on his head. The rest of his body is stewing in a puddle of murky water, back against mildew, the air thick with the smell of rot. He can't stretch his legs, there isn't room enough, and any attempt causes a stabbing sensation so deep and thorough it lingers in the roots of his back molars.

The last he remembers, he was being thrown into the back of a truck amongst sacks of grain stamped USAID: food aid destined for Somalia. Two armed men had leapt into the truck's cabin after him, then bound Adam's hands behind his back and muzzled him with an oily rag. Their faces were concealed but they had the wild eyes and sinewy bodies of *qat* addicts. He began to choke with the pressure of the rag on his tongue and not long after that it went black.

When he eventually awoke, he felt as if his body was suspended on the backs of snails, his limbs dipping into their mucus. A dark circle of sky pulsed above. He punched at the mosquitoes around his head, knocking his hand against a metal bowl. There was bread and some kind of stew, what was left of it, in the bowl. The bread tasted like gasoline, but he ate everything, even licking the bowl's metal rim. The fact that they were feeding him suggested they wanted to keep him alive.

His ID, which they must have seized, reads *Daniel Rainier*. Sofie is the only one at the Awbare camp who knows his real name. She whispers to him: Adam. Just before Sofie cries out though, he has to mouth *Daniel*, lest she bring the roof down with his real name.

It has been years since anyone has called him Adam. In Kenya, he'd done similar work, under a different alias; dangerous work that gave him some way of rationalizing the fact that, unlike most of his colleagues, he didn't have a wife engaged in fundraising for a Kenyan orphanage and two children excelling in international schools in Nairobi. But he didn't have a drinking problem or a penchant for boys, either, which made him something of an anomaly in both the expatriate and aid-working worlds. He'd always been a loner, which suited his work, involving as it did careful movement and a certain unknowability; but at a deeper level, he wasn't actually sure he felt the things that other people felt. At thirty-six, he had never been in love.

He'd been seconded to Ethiopia from Kenya in early 2007, with the escalating violence of al-Shabaab in neighbouring Somalia. Somali refugees were pouring into Jijiga, an Ethiopian town sixty kilometres west of the border, and were being temporarily housed at the reopened UNHCR camp of Awbare: thirteen thousand of them by the time Adam arrived in January, almost forty percent of them children.

His official title at Awbare was "Interim Deputy Logistics Coordinator," but in truth, he was filling in for no one and would not be replaced: he was there on behalf of the State Department, sent to investigate the rumour that militant recruiters posing as refugees had infiltrated the camp.

On his first day, Adam had met with the director of security, Dr. Farhan, who assigned him an interpreter and driver. Mustafa took him on a tour of the facilities, introducing him to various field officers, both local and expatriate. The camp sprawled over several kilometres of rock-strewn desert. The various administrative compounds belonging to international agencies were clustered at the southwest end of the camp. All the camp services—educational, medical, religious, recreational—were located two kilometres to the northeast. Thousands of dome-shaped *aqallo* covered the desert in between, a patchwork quilt of portable dwellings, frames fashioned out of tree boughs and covered with hides, cloth, tarp, plastic bags, scrap metal—whatever could be scavenged. Many of the refugees had brought their homes with them by donkey or camel, traversing some of the most dangerous smuggling routes in the region. For water, people relied upon a series of shallow wells that snaked across the desert.

Mustafa was an animated guide who did not stop talking throughout the tour despite the fact that Adam had stopped listening. In an open-air room at the back of the HIV/AIDS clinic, a petite, olive-skinned woman was leading a breast-feeding workshop. The way she spoke, effortlessly and often with her hands, using Somali mannerisms and gestures, had made Adam want to know how she moved and sounded in English. She cupped her breast at one point—she wore a loose Somali *dirac* covered by an unbuttoned white coat—and although consciously telling himself to look away as Mustafa had respectfully done, he couldn't. She never even glanced in his direction.

Sofie Hadid, Mustafa had told Adam as they walked away from the clinic, led the campaign for access to antiretroviral therapy in the camp. She was a pediatric nurse, specializing in HIV and AIDS.

"How long has she been here?" he asked.

"Years in one camp or another," said Mustafa.

Her first language was Arabic and, while she spoke English with a bit of a lisp, that evaporated, Mustafa said, when she spoke Somali.

Not knowing Arabic had been a distinct disadvantage for Adam in the field. With back-to-back assignments throughout the region over the previous seven years, Adam knew six different ways to say "mosquito" and "no problem," and a smattering of rudimentary Swahili, a language that would be quite useless to him at Awbare. He had never settled in one place long enough to commit to learning its language. He had always been a bit of an adrenalin junkie—restless and quickly dissatisfied, moving between projects, reliant on translators, his cynicism growing in tandem with his salary.

Sofie proved to have a fundamentally different temperament. She genuinely seemed to believe that if she made a difference in one life she'd made a difference in the world. "What choice do we have but to see it this way?" she'd asked him in English with Somali hands.

The months Adam had spent with her had had the measurable effect of slowing him down. Adam had discovered comfort in the sound of another person breathing beside him at night and, at Sofie's request, he no longer slept with a gun.

He lifts his left leg with his hands and leans it against the slick of green wall. His leg has become "it"—lifeless, apart from the pain. He runs his palms down his calves. The break is at the ankle; he can see the protrusion under the blackened skin. He feels the rise of nausea in his throat, and since he can't afford to lose what he's just eaten, he stops his investigation there.

He tries to think through the logistics instead. Daniel Rainier has no family. They won't find the loving and/or rich relatives they must intend to send their demand for ransom.

They will push for his real name, try to beat it out of him. Sofie will report him missing. The camp will be informed. But the ransom won't be paid, even if it comes accompanied by a body part. The US government doesn't officially pay ransom to terrorists. But it does make deals. He thinks of the number of Somalis being held at Guantanamo Bay. Out of your hands, he has to say to himself to stop the circles from growing any wider. Completely out of your hands. Focus on what you can do. Listen, stay sane. Keep that metal bowl—it'll make a good sound when you bang it against the wall or your head. Think about Sofie. She will be thinking about you.

It was Sofie who had suggested they take a break from the camp. He'd been at Awbare for months before there was finally something of a tangible breakthrough. One of the new attendants at the graveyard had apparently been hectoring mourners, lecturing them on proper Islamic burial traditions. While the majority of graveyard visitors, moderate Muslims who had fled from their country because of militant violence, had retreated in fear or quiet anger, there were others who challenged him, enraged by the man's presumption of authority. The ones who concerned Adam, though, were the odd few, all of them young men, who actually stopped to listen.

Adam had kept his eyes on those young men. He saw most of them, after *Isha'a* prayers, slink into a drab-looking *aqal* on the camp's fringes. He watched the traffic in and out of that *aqal* for a week. A thirty-five-year-old religious scholar named Bilal ibn Qadr lived there with his three wives and twelve children. The women were conspicuous in their attempts to be inconspicuous. Unlike the flowing and colourful *duruc* and veils worn by other women in the camp, they wore only the opaquest of black.

The young men who visited every night left the camp under the cover of darkness the following week. Adam reported this far up the food chain. Bilal ibn Qadr was quietly and quickly removed. His wives and children dismantled their *aqal*, accepting the offer of voluntary repatriation.

Adam had taken Sofie to Lamu after that, the jewel of the archipelago just off Kenya's coast. She had never, in all the years she'd been in the region, taken a holiday and Adam wanted to be able to give her this. He had been to Lamu on his first assignment in Kenya years before and had been struck by the beauty of this coast and the elaborate architecture of the town. He wanted to share the beauty of the place with Sofie, but he feared he had spent too much time in this part of the world to see it any longer himself. Beyond its surface, the tensions here were long and deep, the coast tugged between directives issued by Nairobi and foreign interests; the calm of the Swahili coast an uneasy and deceptive one, ripe for exploitation and explosion.

From the balcony of their hotel room, he asked her to describe to him what she saw. She narrowed his focus to what was before them: she pointed at the *dhow* sails fluttering over the water and at pink coral minarets, and she read to him the Arabic inscriptions carved into the wooden doors below. It washed away some of the dirt to see it through her eyes.

"I could live here," she said that night, as they sat on a bougainvillea-draped veranda overlooking the Indian Ocean.

He reached across the table for her hand. "I remember thinking the same thing," he said.

"I wish you still did."

"It's the work. It alters the view."

"Where would you want to live now, if you could choose?"

"I don't know," he said. "I just need to be somewhere I can be useful."

"Let's think of somewhere," she said, "somewhere with a good view."

It was new to him, the idea of imagining life with another person. It touched something in him; a place that emitted a dull, painful glow.

Adam awakes to the muffled relay of one muezzin beginning the call to prayer after another. The air around him wavers in the heat. He can hear a typewriter in the distance, the tickety-tack of fluent fingers, and he wonders how he might enlist the operator to write a letter for him—perhaps he could send it up word by word. Then he feels the keys in his mouth: his teeth are doing the typing, chattering a letter that makes no sense. He's shivering despite the heat, shivering as he sits in a cesspool of sweat, piss and shit; he's become the eye in a cyclone of mosquitoes. *Fuck, fuck, fuck!* he tries to shout.

The effort brings an explosion of tiny stars to his eyes and the small circle above begins to spin. A faceless shadow appears at its edge and chucks something down. A bottle of water hits his good leg. The cap is loose and the water smells rank. I am of more use to them alive than dead, he says to himself, before putting the bottle to his lips.

The shadow above is saying something. He tilts his head toward the sky in order to hear better, but he's stabbed by a sudden pain in the gut and, keeling forward, doesn't so much vomit as throw his insides against the opposite wall.

While they were on holiday on the Kenyan coast someone had left Adam a message. At least, he'd interpreted it as such when he saw it upon his return. A brown handprint had been stamped at eye level on the door to his room. He was living off-site, in a small family-owned hotel in Jijiga's old town, which allowed him more freedom of movement. Mouna left tea outside his door every morning and he had an occasional cigarette with her husband, Abdullah. Most of their talk focused on Abdullah's concern that Adam didn't have a wife.

For some reason he had leaned in to smell the handprint. It had occurred to him that it might be dried blood. The hand of Fatima protects one from the evil eye, he thought in that moment; a thief loses a hand; you extend the right hand to another, not the left; you've got blood on your hands. He felt a rush of bitterness at the back of his throat, that metallic taste one can experience during a long run. A warning, a threat. He opened the door to his room cautiously. He'd left the window open and dust circled in the last sunlight of the day. He packed his few belongings into two duffle bags and messaged Mustafa. When Mustafa pulled up at the back of the hotel after sunset,

Adam dropped the duffle bags out the window. Then he climbed the three storeys down the façade of the building, gripping the window ledges as he lowered himself, balcony by balcony.

He'd had Mustafa take him straight to Sofie's clinic. Sofie was in the back, talking to three women, but stopped speaking as soon as she saw Adam in the doorway. The women turned, immediately lowered their eyes and stood up to leave.

"*As-salamu 'alaykum,*" Adam had mumbled. "I'm sorry, Sofie. Sorry for interrupting."

She waved her hand in some way he couldn't interpret. She exchanged quiet words with each woman in turn, holding their hands in hers as she did. Something serious had transpired in this room.

She closed the door after them and held her finger up to her lips. She watched the women dissolve into the dark between the bars of a glassless window. "Their sons have disappeared," she finally said.

Adam sat down on the edge of a table. The boys had apparently been playing football after school a couple of days ago, nothing out of the ordinary. The ball had been kicked far out of bounds and one of them, Idris, had gone running after it. Two others, Jiinow and Qaalib, had followed. Their classmates had lost sight of them once they'd crossed the road and run round the back of the madrasa. They hadn't been seen since.

Sofie raised her hand, stopping him from saying anything aloud.

"Ten years old," she whispered. "Their mothers are terrified that reporting it will result in some kind of retribution, and they're equally afraid that they will somehow be viewed as suspect by their community."

"What do they want from you?" he asked.

She shrugged. "A witness. I can't really do anything more." Then she looked at him with her eyebrows raised and lips compressed as if to say, *But you can.* And she wasn't wrong—this was why Adam had been seconded here, after all, but there was the matter of the message that had been left on his door. Someone was very likely onto the fact that he had been responsible for ibn Qadr's removal, which meant his cover was compromised. He wasn't sure it was wise to begin investigating anything else at this point. He knew he should busy himself with something innocuous and administrative for the next little while; he should let something very obvious slip past without his noticing in order to ease any suspicions.

But that face of hers. The beauty of it, the imploring. What else could he do?

—

He is licking a cat. No, that can't be right. It takes effort to raise his finger to his mouth to investigate. His teeth seem to have grown fur. He would like more than anything to brush his teeth. A twig like the Somalis use would do.

A sudden explosion of light floods the interior of the well, then thunder booms in the distance. He is thrust back to an August storm, where the cedars by the lake are on fire. His mother says they have to keep an eye on the wind. Adam is terrified, they cannot get out: they have no car anymore because his father drove it over a cliff. Adam runs down to the dock, his mother shouting into his back, he is yanking at the canoe, not strong enough, only six, and his mother is shouting: "Adam, Addie, baby, what are you doing, this isn't the time for this," and he says, "but, but," and points at the fire now behind the cabin, and she turns her head and then runs to him, hauls him up by the armpits, drops him into the canoe, heaves it into the water, and with one foot in she pushes it off the rock, jumps in and collapses. They are floating. And the world all around them is on fire.

Another crack of thunder, this one so close that pebbles begin to fall and the wall behind Adam vibrates. He can hear the pepper of gunfire and shouting above. A body rappels down into the well. The body barks, yanks his arm, tries to pull him upright, but Adam's legs won't work—one is dead, the other liquid. The body shouts, objects pummel them from above, he holds his arms up as the body works, shoving and grunting, until Adam is harnessed to the body and they are rising inch by inch out of the well. He is floating and the world above is on fire. He sees a horizon of orange flame before a sack is brought down over his head. The smell of wheat and burning oil engulfs him. He hears the volley of gunfire as he is lifted and shoved into a box. The back of another truck, the wheels spinning until they gain traction, the truck lurching into the desert night.

There is a compulsion in movement, despite all the un-known: the promise of somewhere else has always been, for

Adam, the promise of being someone else. He's never stopped long enough to ask himself whether that promise has ever actually borne out. Perhaps that's the point, though: you migrate from one dangerous situation to another, your Spidey-Sense on high alert, your wits, mettle and resourcefulness at the fore and the more existential questions retreat somewhere beyond reach or consideration. But then one day, you find yourself in love, and the next day, you are kidnapped.

When he wakes, he feels the coolness of concrete beneath him. The sun is rising, the view from inside the sack over his head mutating from black to brown to rust. He fingers the edge of the burlap at his chest, realizing he can lift it. He keeps his eyes closed against the sudden assault of light as he pulls the sack off his head, and manages to push himself up into a sitting position.

"My friend," says a voice to his left.

The slightest turn of his head makes him nauseous. He squints against the light bouncing off walls of an alarming blue not found in nature. There is a small window behind thick plaster lattice about ten feet from the ground. In the opposite corner of the room, a man sits cross-legged, his hair and beard such light grey they are almost white, his folded limbs long and pale like those of a praying mantis.

"Where are we?" Adam manages, his voice a hoarse whisper.

"Sometimes I can smell the sea," says the man. "My grandfather was a whaler. My father was in the oil industry, worked offshore. The sea has given the Norwegians everything. So the fact that I smell the sea might not mean anything except that I am Norwegian."

Adam is exhausted by so many words.

"You've got malaria," the man says. "You're the colour of piss."

Jaundice. Of course. His hand rises to touch his face. "How long have you been here?" he asks.

"Three hundred and thirty-six days," says the man, trilling his r's.

Three hundred and something days in a year—he cannot, in this moment, remember the exact number.

"When did they capture you, Adam?"

Hearing his real name brings his heart into his throat. "Daniel," he says. "My name's Daniel."

"Sorry. You told me Adam when I asked last night."

Adam points a finger to his temple; his brain is obviously messed up.

The Norwegian nods. "I was sick for weeks." He leans forward and picks up a flip-flop, then whacks it against the concrete. He tweezes something from the floor with his thumb and forefinger. He walks over to Adam's corner with a flat brown thing in his hand and says: "I'm convinced this is what cured me."

Adam looks into the man's palm. A squashed cockroach.

"Think about it," the Norwegian says. "They live in the dirtiest places on earth. They must have some kind of immunity to the usual bacteria and parasites." He pops the thing into his mouth, crunches it between his molars and grimaces as he swallows. "It's not so bad if you wash it down with tea. They bring tea four times a day," he says, nodding at the door frame.

There is no door. There is a hallway painted bubble-gum pink. Adam can smell incense burning somewhere, hear voices, male.

"Who are they?" he asks.

"Children," the Norwegian says. "Children with AK-47s and some fantasy of virgins in the afterlife."

"Do you know what they want?"

"One million dollars," he says with a small mocking laugh. He becomes more subdued then. "I rather suspect my currency has just been devalued."

Adam shakes his head, not understanding. Euro or krone, which do they use in Norway?

"An American has to be worth a great deal more to them."

Adam isn't clear-headed enough to conduct a realistic assessment of the Norwegian. Is that bitterness or resignation in his voice? Is it all Americans he resents or just present company?

A boy in short brown pants and a fraying white T-shirt kicks his flip-flops off in the doorway and shuffles into the room carrying a tray. He is alone, unmasked, unarmed. He is a child. Perhaps only nine or ten. What could he possibly know about virgins in the afterlife?

"Abdi," the Norwegian says with some apparent affection, taking the tray from him. The glasses clink as he sets the tray down on the floor and it occurs to Adam that they could smash those glasses and take the boy hostage. But then what?

"Do you take sugar?" the Norwegian asks Adam.

The improbable civility of the moment allows Adam to imagine, briefly, that they are simply fellow expats sharing a pleasant exchange on the balcony of a small hotel on the Red Sea, Abdi, their waiter, hovering nearby for a tip.

The Norwegian reaches again for his flip-flop and brings it with a whack to the floor. He hands Adam a little amuse-bouche to wash down with tea. The tea is so viscous and sweet Adam thinks he could swallow a rock this way if he had to. The cockroach slips down his throat. He attempts to straighten his bad leg with both hands, wincing with the slightest movement. The Norwegian offers Adam the pillow he is sitting upon to prop up his leg and helps Adam straighten it as much as the pain will permit. The Norwegian studies his ankle, probing it with his fingertips, and says the tibia needs realigning. "I can do it if you'd like," he offers.

"Are you a doctor?"

"Aren't we all doctors in Africa?"

True enough, thinks Adam. He had to pull out an aid worker's bad tooth once, but the idea of having his leg realigned makes him distinctly queasy.

"You'll walk with a limp for the rest of your life otherwise."

Adam suspects the damage might already be done, but he bites his bottom lip and nods.

The Norwegian kneels at his feet and lifts the pillow supporting Adam's ankle onto his thighs. "Count backwards from ten in Swahili," he says.

At *sita*, there is a crunch and a bolt of lightning rips through Adam's body. The Norwegian muffles his scream with his palm and Adam sees navy, navy for miles, a smattering of stars and then black.

It is night when he wakes again, weak green shadows marking the floor. His leg is still elevated upon the pillow. There is a glass of tea, a banana and a round lump of hard bread at his feet. Adam hears whispering in the room and sees the outline of the Norwegian on his knees with his forehead to the floor. He is praying, praying the Muslim way.

—

Adam has managed, this morning, to pull himself up onto one foot. He is standing propped up against the wall, a little breathless, very weak, the edges of his vision smeared with Vaseline. He can't see through the latticed window, but he imagines that if he were back to his normal strength, he could jump and grip the ledge and pull himself up high enough to look out.

Oskar—his name is Oskar, Adam finally thought to ask—is telling him to go easy.

"They'll be wanting to make a video soon," he says. "They'll have you telling your family and friends at home that you are fine, but of course you won't be fine for long unless they pay your ransom."

They first recorded Oskar eleven months ago. They made a second video five months later, but for that one they had him wear a black glove on his left hand in order to suggest it had been amputated.

"Why didn't they just cut it off?"

"I think they'd grown rather fond of me," he says. "It was different before you arrived—we played cards together sometimes—totally *haram*, but there you go. The boys are just as trapped as we are."

"Maybe they're kinder because you're Muslim."

"If you can't beat them . . ." He shrugs. "Isn't that how the expression goes? It structures the day," Oskar adds, suddenly pensive.

Why haven't his family and friends paid the ransom? Adam wonders. Oskar tells him he has two teenaged daughters in Bergen who have recently gone to live with their aunt because their mother, his first wife, is mentally unstable. He has a father with dementia and a French girlfriend in Nairobi who is all of twenty-six. Given all Adam's years based out of Nairobi, he's surprised they have never crossed paths.

"Do you have children?" Oskar asks.

Adam shakes his head. "A girlfriend but no, no children."

"Nephews, nieces?"

He shakes his head again.

"Your poor parents."

"They're both dead, I'm afraid."

"All the more reason you should have children. There will be no legacy of you and your people once you're gone."

"I was a sperm donor in my late twenties," Adam finds himself saying. He's never actually told anyone this before. "Paid my way through the end of graduate school that way."

"So you might be a father, then."

Adam disagrees. "A father is a man who is present in your life," he says. He'd had longer relationships with some of his mother's colleagues than he'd had with his own father. What matters, in Adam's opinion, is that you stick around.

"What if one day some offspring comes looking for you?"

Adam remembers thinking about that at that time. The clinic asked you to consider whether you wanted to disclose your identity when a child turned eighteen. Most donors don't. Adam was one of those most—why complicate life for everyone involved? He sees himself as someone who simply went some small way toward helping people who wanted to become parents. And they helped him by paying him for a supply of something he has wasted plenty of in his life.

"And your girlfriend, what does she think of this?"

"Sofie? It hasn't come up."

Adam had asked her early on if she wanted children—he'd wondered, given how many she had seen die. She shrugged and said that while she felt an occasional longing, she just didn't think the world needed more children. You can't really do the kind of work either of them does with children—and for both of them, that work matters most.

Oskar looks amused. "My driver in Mogadishu is one of forty-three," he says. "The forty-second of his father's forty-three children. A very famous sheikh. Three wives. Imagine what he could have done with four."

"I thought you were based in Nairobi."

"Most of the time, yes," he says, offering nothing more.

Adam turns his concentration to placing his other foot flat on the floor. Oskar's adjustment and a day of elevation have reduced the swelling considerably, but his foot looks like a piece of rotten meat. Fuck, he thinks, what if it's gangrenous? He's seen this before in diabetics. There's a way of treating gangrene with maggots; letting them eat the dead flesh away. Eating cockroaches and being fed upon by maggots—could it get any worse than this? He supposes it could.

Abdi has arrived with tea and porridge. He looks alarmed at the sight of Adam standing upright and hangs back with the tray, hesitant. Adam would like to be able to reassure Abdi that he is no threat. What sense can a child make of a situation like this?

"Thank you," Adam says in English.

Abdi hands Oskar the tray and scuttles off.

"What's his story?" Adam asks Oskar.

"He's an orphan. Saw his parents killed by government forces. An easy recruit."

Perhaps the same would have been true of Adam if he'd grown up like Abdi. Lured by some alternative, any alternative, to the emptiness.

"Here," says Oskar, holding out a bowl, "come and eat."

Adam's appetite appears to have returned. He shovels porridge into his mouth with his right hand; sorghum and sour buttermilk. Oskar, meanwhile, eats slowly, with long pauses between each bite. He fills in the pauses by telling Adam what he knows about the hierarchy of things here. There's a house leader, Faisal, who gives Abdi and six other teenagers directions. Faisal isn't much more than a teenager himself. He reports to a slightly older man they call the Mullah. The Mullah travels with a posse of four armed men in their twenties. Oskar knows when they are arriving: he can differentiate between vehicles by the sounds of their engines. "I'm a mechanical engineer," he offers by way of explanation. "They've even called upon me to fix their vehicles a couple of times."

It strikes Adam that this might have presented an opportunity for Oskar to do something subversive, rig the engine in some way that might cause it to explode, but Oskar seems strangely resigned to his place here.

"What's it like out there?" Adam asks.

He shrugs. "Not much to see. Four or five white buildings like this. A cinderblock wall topped with barbed wire surrounding them all. A well. Chickens, goats. Some women, children."

"A family compound?"

"All Somalis are family."

"What about beyond the wall?"

"Too high to see. Just a lot of sky."

A lot of sky. Adam's mother had to bring him with her to the scene of the accident. He was only five; she couldn't leave him alone at home. The police needed her to look down into the valley and identify the car. Adam stayed back with another officer, looking up rather than down. There was a vast empty blue without horizon, which made him feel the world was a vast and empty place. He remembers wondering, then, how humans had been created. How and why. His father had driven over the cliff quite deliberately, Adam knew it even then, nobody needed to tell him, nobody needed to lie.

The summer after his father killed himself Adam's mother insisted they go to the cabin by the lake as they did every summer. They didn't have a car any longer—in fact, his mother would never have one again—so they'd taken a bus and then a taxi she'd arranged to bring them into the woods. And that July the forest had caught fire. There was horizon to the sky Adam saw from the middle of the lake, a horizon of fire, and it was hard not to feel they were the last people on earth as the world was ending.

TESS

I'M RENTING the top-floor apartment of a small brick house with a huge view. It's become a home over these past few weeks, with its clunky hand-built wooden furniture, the tentative electricity, the lace doilies on every available surface, the generosity of my landlady Elysia's interruptions, always bringing me something to eat or drink.

From the terrace, with its succulents and geraniums in terracotta pots, Spinalonga, the former leper colony I have been mapping, looks like a tumble of beige rocks rising from the sea. On this shore, the dusty coastal road snakes its way up a parched hillside at the western edge of the bay.

Directly across the road from Elysia's house is the bar, the commentary of a football match invariably spilling out its door. Elysia warned me about the place when I first arrived. "Not for ladies," she said, and I laughed.

No one could mistake me for a lady. When my cousin Stavros came to visit shortly after my arrival, he took one look at me and immediately suggested we go to the bar.

Stavros is my father's older brother's son. He is a few years older than me, and has a vague recollection of meeting me as a child, when my father, siblings and I spent a summer in Plaka with our common grandparents. Stavros is one of only a few relatives left in Crete on either of my parents' sides, everyone having died, or been driven to Athens or further abroad a generation ago in search of better prospects.

My father has been encouraging me to make this trip ever since my separation from Emily. *Go see the family. Show the boy his roots*—the boy being his grandson, my son, Max. I'm planning to fly back to Toronto at the end of June and bring Max out here for a few weeks. In the meantime, this break has given me the time I needed to start research on a new project I'm calling "Geographies of Isolation." It will be a comparative study of three abandoned communities, starting with the ruins on the rocky island I can see out the window of Elysia's third-storey apartment right now.

As Stavros and I walked over the road to the bar that first night of our reacquaintance, I had to correct him, "It's Tess now, not Teresa." I followed him through an ugly, olive-green room with a large-screen TV, men drinking and smoking away at small tables—and out onto a terrace on stilts above the lapping water.

After the waiter brought us menus, Stavros told me not to order fish; it was all frozen, flown in from Thailand. "They used to fish with dynamite," he said, lobbing an imaginary explosive over his shoulder toward the water.

I pictured the contents of the ocean floating dead on its surface. Eels and whales and corals and seaweeds, hitherto unknown species from the ocean depths, our evolutionary history thrown belly-up. "Holy shit," I said, in lieu of anything else to say.

He nodded and said: "We are shit."

I assumed he meant all of us—as a species.

Stavros is a chef himself, chef and proprietor of one of the most popular restaurants in nearby Elounda. There are days when his restaurant is besieged by the exodus off cruise ships. His hands are large, his nails trimmed short and tidy, his silvering beard short and tidy as well, and when he leaned in that evening with a knife and fork to delicately debone the quail we had ordered, I could smell the pepper and woodsmoke of his kitchen and cologne.

He wanted me to know he was a worldly man, "not like those peasants," he said, pointing toward the men in the bar. He'd lived in Athens with his first wife for several years and he'd travelled: England, France. I think all this was code for *I've met a gay person before, and I'm okay with it, but those guys out there? Maybe not so much.*

A few years ago, Stavros married a Swedish tourist twenty-five years younger than him. He is now the proud fifty-six-year-old father of three children under five. We may be shit, but we keep on carrying on. I don't even want to imagine the energy having three small children at his age requires; having one child in my forties takes it out of me.

I told Stavros about Max, who will be eight in the fall.

"He has a father?" Stavros asked tentatively.

"Two mothers," I said. "Although we're not together."

"Okay, okay," Stavros said, nodding.

Whatever his confusion, as soon as I returned with Max at the beginning of July, Stavros had scooped him right up and plunked him on his shoulders like Max was one of his own. Stavros speaks to him in Greek, wanting him to pick up the language, which I encourage.

This afternoon, Elysia's daughter has taken Max down to the village beach with her kids, leaving me to do some work. I move my laptop out to the table on the terrace, nudging the plug into an extension cord held together with tape. I'm transcribing interviews I've done with the majority of the village elders, the hours and hours of recordings I made in June when the Meltemi winds were so relentless it was impossible to make the crossing to Spinalonga.

It's hard to focus, though; I'm missing these moments with my son. In the time we have been apart, Max has grown more into his features and I have a clearer picture of the man he will become. He's lost the roundness of his younger face, and the dimples he shares with me and my brother have become more pronounced. He has my father's long, lean build and Emily's colouring—her dark brown hair and hazel eyes. He has an explosive laugh much like mine.

Restless to see Max, I make my way outside, past the red, white and blue fishing boats, their wooden traps empty, dozens of squid skewered onto wooden stakes drying in the sun.

The beach is a small, sloping stretch covered in stones. The old man who cooks in the bar at night waves at me from the terrace of the beachside café. He orders two glasses of retsina and clinks his glass against mine. He was kind about my Greek at the beginning, but now he teases me, says I sound like I'm chewing undercooked potatoes.

Max comes bounding across the rocks with the bare feet of a child who doesn't register discomfort. He wants to show me the remains of some desiccated octopus he has found on the beach and the old man starts to tell him about a past when the sea was thick with octopi and other creatures. What other creatures? Max wants to know. Since he doesn't know all the words in English, the cook fetches a pencil and a paper menu and starts to sketch various fish on the back in quite elaborate detail.

We wander back up the road as the sun is setting a brilliant red. Lamb is roasting over a charcoal brazier, filling the air with garlic and rosemary. Stavros and his wife have already arrived with their little ones: she is breastfeeding the baby while the other two tear about. Max and I dash upstairs to wash off the sand and the sea and I can hear the music starting up as I turn off Max's shower.

"Sebastian is allergic to water," Max says, as I towel off his lean brown body.

"I don't think that's possible, buddy."

"But it is! Mama and I looked it up on Google."

"It must be very rare. I wonder what happens when he cries."

"He doesn't—not even when he whacked his tooth out on the monkey bars. He got ten bucks for that one, Mom, ten bucks!"

"Well, I guess his mother can afford that with what she saves on swimming lessons," I say, tapping one leg as I get him into a pair of shorts.

Down in the courtyard, Elysia and her daughter are laying the table. Soon it is covered in plates of lamb, rice, potatoes, feta and warm olives, and bowls of various greens collected in the nearby hills. Stavros offers a toast to family and friends before settling in beside me with a plate of food. Nico, Elysia's son-in-law, regales everyone with a story about the ridiculous way people coddle their dogs in Athens.

Stavros has promised Max he'll teach him how to play chess after dinner, but by that time Max has fallen asleep on a lawn chair. Someone has covered him with a blanket. I can't believe Max can sleep through the noise, his face illuminated by the strings of Christmas lights hanging from the trellis above.

I lie down on the lawn chair beside my boy and check my phone. There's a text from Emily wanting to talk to Max, but it's too late for that tonight. I do the dutiful co-parenting thing, though, and send a couple of photos, one where Max is pretending to stab a jellyfish.

"A little aggressive," Emily texts back in response.

I roll my eyes. I was stung by a jellyfish the first time I went swimming here and since telling Max the story he's been determined to avenge the harm inflicted upon me. *Let him be a boy*, I want to text back, but I don't bother. I let Max roughhouse and take more physical risks than she does, which has resulted in stitches more than once, and a broken wrist, and Emily yelling: "Have you noticed that the only times he ends up in Emergency are when he's with you?"

God, I look forward to the day when Emily is no longer the judge of my parenting skills.

—

This morning, Stavros is taking us over to Spinalonga in his boat. I've been here numerous times throughout the summer to map the former colony, usually paying one of the fishermen to taxi me over. No one from the mainland comes here, but increasingly, the island is an optional side trip for tourists on the cruise ships that harbour in Elounda. There are still some local rumours about the place, superstitions attached to it—on a still day in just the right conditions, people say you can sometimes hear a woman wailing—but in a practical sense the residents of Plaka actually thrived during the years of the colony's existence, supplying it with labour, building materials and food.

The water is a bit choppy today, so Stavros keeps his hand overtop of Max's as he lets him steer. It only takes about ten minutes to get round to the northern shore. When Stavros was a teenager, he and his friends used to come out here and dare each other to jump from the highest point into the water. I've asked Stavros not to tell Max this story.

We pull up to the jetty on the northern shore, where the stone archways mark the entrance to the Venetian fortress that predated the leper colony. What strikes me about this place every time is the silence, just the buzz of insects, the twitter of tiny birds and the lapping of water against the shore.

We tread softly down the gravel paths and through buildings in various states of disrepair. The local authority has done a reasonable job of posting signs in Greek and English to indicate former uses. We pass a dormitory, sanitarium, washhouse and kitchen. Stavros makes the sign of the cross before the church and whispers a brief prayer familiar to me from the Sunday mornings of my childhood.

Max has zero interest in the buildings. The graveyard merits a grunt of "cool," but what he really wants to do is fish. Once we have found a good spot for him to cast his rod, Stavros produces a picnic of bread and cheese and olives and wine, laying it out on a linen placemat. He is a gentleman and a bit of a romantic. We sit in the shade on a flat slab of rock looking out at the water while Max and his rod fight the wind.

"This is all one really needs to live, isn't it," I say.

Stavros nods. "The food and the sun and the sea and the love," he says. He lies down with his arms under his head and looks up at the cloudless sky. "You know, my first wife, she died of cancer," he says after a contemplative minute.

Ovarian, I assume, given how he places his hand on his lower stomach. "I'm sorry, Stavros. How long ago?"

"Seven years."

"Were you together for a long time?"

"Since school," he says.

"Four times she was pregnant," he says. "But four times she lost the baby."

"That must have been really hard for you both."

He nods slowly. "But then I get a chance for three more," he says. "You never know with life. He surprises you."

"He certainly does."

I'd been ambivalent about having children. The first time it came up was when I was visiting Emily in DC, about six months into our relationship. She'd been living for years on the top floor of an old Victorian house owned by an older lesbian couple, Annie and Marlene. They'd raised a son, Annie's son from an earlier marriage to a man, a boy who was now a father himself. We'd had dinner, the four of us, their daughter-in-law dropping by at some point with their grandson. I'd watched Emily smoosh her lips into little Sam's forehead and reached for her hand.

"I want that," she had later whispered, her head on my shoulder, lying on a mattress under the sloping ceiling of her bedroom on the top floor. "I want that with you. To be a family."

Apart from a sister in Chicago, Emily was estranged from her family. Her mother and stepfather were fundamentalist Christians and had no place in their church or hearts for her. Even her sister, who had left the church, was of the "don't ask don't tell" school.

"That would be nice," I managed to whisper.

I had never even considered having children, never wanted them. My own mother hadn't been mentally robust enough to handle being a parent, leaving my father with far too much to deal with. And as a woman, if you have any ambition in academia? Even in the best circumstances, I've seen female colleagues lose their footing on the ladder once they have children; you can't slip down a rung, especially without a permanent job—it is a brutal climb as it is.

Emily had moved to Toronto later that year. We managed to cobble together enough for a down payment on a house in a neighbourhood of small, detached postwar bungalows. Soon after we moved in, we heard that a Starbucks would be taking over the old bank building around the corner. More than one bungalow on our street was sold to a developer once that news was out. Maybe it was contagious, but Emily started talking about wanting to add a second floor to accommodate a baby only a month after we'd moved in.

I had been planning to do some work on the house myself during the summer, but nothing as ambitious as an additional floor. I asked her if we could please just wait a year, until I had tenure.

She was almost thirty-four, and had buried herself in studies that showed how dramatically female fertility falls off after thirty-five. No matter how much I tried to rationalize away averages and get her to focus on the range instead, she only became more anxious and insistent. She found a fertility doctor recommended by a colleague and set up an appointment for us, "just for a preliminary consultation."

I was feeling under so much pressure at the time, putting all the pieces together for the tenure review that would take place at the end of the spring term, that I reacted badly.

"This is not just about me," she yelled, "this is about *us*, our life together, our future."

"So is getting tenure," I said. "I want us to be secure. I can't take on any more risk without that."

"You really do sound like an investment advisor some-times," she said.

There were times when she said that was one of the things she loved about me. My practical side, my planning.

But this was not one of those times.

"This is supposed to be something beautiful," she said, her voice breaking.

I felt undone in the face of her tears. I put my arms around her and said we could meet the doctor for a consultation, but then we really would have to wait a year—"not even a year," I said, "maybe nine or ten months."

"The length of time it takes to have a baby."

"Look, if you're that worried about your eggs, you could have some of them frozen."

Of course, we didn't know then that there would be compli-cations. "Has anyone ever told you that you have endometrio-sis?" was how Dr. Erskine began the conversation after Emily had done a number of routine tests.

"No," Emily said, the worry evident in her voice.

"You must have very painful periods."

"Yes," she said.

"And that's been the case for a long time?"

"Since my twenties, I'd say."

Dr. Erskine pulled out a laminated chart of the female reproductive system then and began to trace the extent of the problem with her finger.

"There are surgical options that could increase the likelihood of conceiving," said Dr. Erskine, sliding a pamphlet across the table, but Emily was still staring at the chart, not really registering what she was being told.

"Are you telling me I can't have a baby?" she finally said.

"There is some endometrial tissue around the ovaries in addition to the blockage in one of the fallopian tubes. Without surgery, I would say your chances are very, very slim."

"And with surgery?"

"A little less so."

Emily was grey and inert.

"We have a counsellor on staff," said Dr. Erskine, standing up. "I could see if she might be available for a few minutes. I'll be right back."

One entire wall of Dr. Erskine's office was covered with photos of babies conceived with the help of the clinic. Fat pink and brown babies, notes of thanks with hearts and fancy lettering below them.

"I just want to go home," said Emily.

I had to lift her out of the chair. I draped her arm around my shoulder and put my arm around her waist, and walked for both of us.

Emily felt her body had betrayed her and she wondered if she was being punished for some reason. Emily, buoyant, optimistic Emily, was gone. The transformation in her scared me. I asked her if we should look into surgery, or whether she might want to talk to that counsellor at the clinic; I asked her if she'd ever consider adoption. I had to teach, I had to go to work; I would bring her a cup of tea in bed in the morning and it would still be sitting there beside her, untouched, when I got home at the end of the day.

I felt as if so many cracks were appearing in the foundation that everything might collapse. I couldn't bear it, I had to fix it.

"I have eggs," I said one night, sitting down on the end of our bed. "Our eggs. And a uterus. They just happen to be in me."

I'd made it sound so simple. The reality was so much more complicated. I'd thought it through in very practical and clinical terms; I'd never imagined having the reactions I did. To begin with, I couldn't bring myself to entertain the idea of being inseminated, even by a female doctor armed with a syringe. It wasn't an ideological or political stance, but a deep, visceral aversion to being penetrated—and, even worse, to the idea of something living being unleashed inside me.

I wanted to do IVF instead. Have the comingling occur outside of me. But I had no idea that the cocktail of hormones we'd be jabbing into my abdomen in order to hyperstimulate my ovaries was going to make me feel crazy. That I would cry for hours, be overwhelmed with anxiety and have to take an Ativan just to endure the assault of a transvaginal ultrasound.

The doctor extracted seven eggs over the course of two cycles, which produced four implantable embryos—two of which were transferred into me, one of which took hold and became Max, the other quietly fading away. We had the remaining two put into cryopreservation since Emily still hoped that with surgery, she might one day be able to carry a child. At the time I agreed to this, I just wanted to stop crying. Emily was the crier. I hated the total lack of control over my feelings. We were paying $10,000 a month for this privilege of turning me into someone I didn't know.

And then there were those nine months. I'd always been able to flatten my breasts with a sports bra, but there was nothing I could do to contain them when I became pregnant. I would tell myself this was temporary, in the service of something bigger, but I would imagine ripping away the fat and the flesh and hurling it into space. The idea of having a double mastectomy when it was all over set in around the seventh month.

At least my belly grew hard—if I thought of it like a shell, I could turn it into something beautiful, imagining a pearl growing inside. It was both mine and not mine, a formerly uninhabited space now home to someone, and this made it easier, particularly once Max started knocking back. *Hey little buddy*, I would say as he shifted around inside, hoofing me in the diaphragm or the ribs.

I had a Caesarian; the swiftest exit. I couldn't bring myself to breastfeed. Excruciating as it was, I bound those bloated breasts in defiance of both the midwife and Emily—I just wanted to shut that whole part of the operation down as quickly as possible.

And yet for all that ambivalence and pain and hard work, here we are. Look at that extraordinary creature throwing his fishing line out into the water, his grandparents' village gleaming white in the distance. I've heard women say that they have trouble getting their heads around the fact that their bodies produced boys, but I have no such trouble. His existence makes sense of mine.

—

I'm sitting out on the terrace, having put Max to bed, drinking a glass of Nico's questionable red wine. Scattered lights are twinkling along the shore, all the way to Elounda. We'll be home in two days, and I already feel the relative freedoms of the summer evaporating.

I'd tried to push some simmering anxiety aside as Max and I took the bus into Elounda today for a final meal at Stavros's restaurant. He had closed it to customers in order to cook a special lunch for the two of us, bringing one plate at a time. Warm olives with rosemary, a piece of feta flaked with oregano and drizzled in smoky oil, a circle of *taramosalata*, an accordion of grilled calamari, roasted pigeon, a plate of potatoes, carrots and green beans.

"Did I ever tell you Pappouli used to kill pigeons with a slingshot when he was a kid?" I asked Max.

"Whoa," he said, his eyes growing wide.

"He would take them home to his mother and she would pluck and roast them for lunch."

"I wonder if Stavros killed this one with a slingshot."

"You'll have to ask him."

Stavros joined us at the end of the meal, bringing me a glass of ouzo. I was so full and it was so hot and still that my eyelids were closing. Max and Stavros were talking about slingshots and Stavros asked if we wanted to see this afternoon's football match at the stadium.

"Do you guys mind if I don't join you?" I said. "I think I need a nap."

"Come," Stavros gestured, leading us through the restaurant and the kitchen behind and into the small enclosed courtyard at the back. The walls were white, the flowers purple, and a thousand lemon rinds covered the tiled ground, drying in the sun. Stavros pointed at the hammock hanging between the kitchen wall and a squat tree.

So now Max is exhausted from the day but I'm wide awake thanks to the hours in that hammock. Emily has just messaged me, once again too late to talk to Max.

Actually it was you I wanted to talk to, she texts in reply.

In my experience, this usually means Emily is about to ask for something. *Can it wait until I get back?* I text back.

No, she says. *I wanted to let you know I have an appointment at the fertility clinic tomorrow. I'm going to try and have a baby.*

I lean back so hard that I hear the wooden slats of my chair cracking. She wants to have a baby? At this point? At her age? What about her fertility issues? What about her new job? She's finally just gone back to work after all these years.

Are you planning on using the same donor? I finally text Emily back.

Tess—I'm going to use our embryos so that Max has a full genetic sibling. It was the plan.

She's timed this deliberately—dropped a bomb when I'm at too much of a distance to do anything about it. It takes months to get in to see Dr. Erskine.

Don't you think I have a right to some say in what happens to the embryos?

I don't think you have any right to tell me whether or not I can have a child.

She's waited until the last possible moment to tell me. There isn't any time for me to object, any way for me to intervene. But I do object. With every fibre of my complicated being.

LILA

STANDING AT the streetcar stop on my way in to work, I see my sweater lying at the edge of the road, evidence of last night's bad behaviour. There had been a lineup outside the bar across the street to hear a band play. I'd turned off the lights in my apartment and paced in front of the window, slurping back one tumbler of wine after another before the ice cubes even had a chance to melt. The line soon started to snake through the door. The windows had been thrown open despite the winter night and a burst of rockabilly recast the street into a small town in a warmer place. I continued to stare out the window, not pacing so much as hovering by then, an alien from some faraway country studying the ways of this place and its people.

At some point I had walked across the street and into the bar. Most of the crowd were crushed up by the stage at the back at this point, listening to the band. I took the lone stool left at the bar and ordered a double vodka on ice. And then I heard the incongruous sound of a dog barking and twisted to the left, my elbow slipping off the bar. There was a man standing there, he was tall, kind of scruffy, and he had a giant German shepherd by his side. I remember asking him his dog's name. It was Maggie. Maybe he told me his name as well, I can't remember. He started to bottle-feed his dog a beer. I had another drink, one at least, but I don't remember getting home.

A Chinese woman looking for empty liquor bottles is now poking my sweater with a stick.

There's nowhere to sit on the streetcar, and feeling a little shaky on my feet, I press the side of my face against a window, which both steadies me and cools half of my flushed face.

I'm late for work and Mirabelle and her supervisor, Leslie, are already in Jacqui's office for our meeting. "I'm really sorry," I say, rushing in.

The pleasantries quickly fade and the questions begin. I've been working with Robin for almost three months now—can I say I am any closer to being able to help identify who she is?

"Given some of the music she's drawn to—"

"—so we're doing music therapy now?" Leslie interrupts.

It strikes me, and certainly not for the first time, how many well-meaning women enter this profession and lose more of their optimism to cynicism each year. What kind of mentoring do they provide for the next generation? For women like Mirabelle, who is probably only in her mid-twenties, a woman who has not liked me from the start.

"There are more than enough CBT elements to the work we're doing with Robin to satisfy the agency," Jacqui says, intervening.

"Listen, the thing is, we're getting somewhere," I say. "I wouldn't recommend moving her right now. It would be really disruptive for her."

"We think she could benefit from socializing with others her own age before she starts school in January," says Mirabelle. "A group home will provide that, along with therapy and some instruction in basic life skills."

I can't help myself: "I don't think this is about what she needs at all," I say.

Jacqui leans forward, taking charge. "We're going to request that you bring an interim assessment from us forward to your next case report meeting before any decisions are made. We'll have that to you by Friday afternoon at the latest."

Jacqui sees the women out to the waiting room, while I hover behind in her office. She returns and closes the door.

"Lila?" is all she says.

"They just want to shunt her from one part of the system to another where she's no longer their responsibility."

"I think it's likely that they can't extend her stay in emergency foster care any longer. What I'm wondering is whether seeing Robin go into a group home would be too disruptive for *you*."

A wash of heat comes over me.

"Do you need me to take over?" she asks.

"No," I say, as tears tumble down my face. I wipe my nose with the back of my hand. "I can handle it."

Her lips are drawn in a tight straight line, a look of inscrutability I haven't seen directed at me in some time.

She had been willing to give me a chance all those years ago. My license was still under suspension when I'd come back to Jacqui to talk to her about the possibility of a job. She'd asked me why I'd been suspended. I told her that I'd come dangerously close to a romantic involvement with a client. The principal accusation Izzie's mother had levelled against me, after all, was that I had been having an affair with her daughter's father. This had allowed me to put the father, rather than the child, at the centre of the story.

Jacqui hired me once I had fulfilled the disciplinary requirements to have my license reinstated. I had additional training, saw a counsellor, and did voluntary work on a research project, working with data rather than clients. I told Jacqui that I'd rather not work with parents and their children for a little while. Her one condition was that I stick to a weekly meeting of AA.

In the bathroom, I run both taps in some futile attempt to cover up the sound as I throw up into the toilet. These walls have heard it all before. The slap of a heroin addict searching for a vein, the smash of someone's face against the metal paper towel dispenser, the quiet moan of a cutter on the job.

Just get through the day, I tell myself, looking into the warped tin mirror over the sink. I wash my face and run my fingers over the smudge of yesterday's mascara. My eyes are bloodshot, the skin beneath them blue.

I know with certainty that if I were to suggest fostering Robin, it would raise serious questions. I would no longer be seen as impartial. Leslie would probably refer Robin to another social worker in order to assess my claims of progress. My failure to get closer to identifying who she is might even be construed as an act of deliberate obstruction. And if they want dirt, no digging is required: it's all down in my record. I would lose her. And she would lose me. And neither of us wants that.

She could have turned around to those old ladies on the bus and told them exactly who she was. Instead, she said nothing to them and leaned into me. She feels safer with me than wherever she has come from. If she requires my collusion to keep her safe, to keep her with me, then she has it.

You can handle this, I say to myself in the mirror.

But I can't go back to my apartment. I travel up Bathurst to my mother's building instead. In her condo, I stare out the window of the solarium, a grid of city lights, and try to picture the geography of eastern Europe. Robin and I come from opposite sides of the Black Sea: Romania on the west, Georgia on the east. But what do I know about either place beyond some common water and Soviet occupation? I once heard a Georgian choir perform: women's voices, polyphonic, piercing, dissonant. They may well have been singing about flowers poking their heads through snow on sunny mountainsides, but to me, it had sounded like women in mourning.

I do a search online for common Georgian phrases, and find a script that looks like it is made up of broken hearts. I attempt to pronounce the Georgian words for *hello, goodbye* and *how are you*. In the top right-hand corner of the next page

I land on, I find Robin's flower-sun-pinwheel—a *borjgali*, apparently, an ancient symbol of the sun. I catch my breath. She had given me this clue weeks ago; she'd wanted me to figure it out. And that clue is now lying quite nakedly in my office. I will fold it up and put it in my briefcase in the morning, bring it home.

I have the thought that if Robin were the one to suggest me as a foster parent, her case workers might listen. But how can that emerge without words, and without it seeming, more importantly, like I have planted the idea in her mind?

In the middle of the night, unable to sleep, I turn on the light in the closet and pull out the box of my mother's marble eggs. I unwrap the newspaper around them and lay them on the floor. There are twelve of them, each a different colour. I choose the most flawless of them all, the white alabaster one without seams, rewrap it and nudge it into my briefcase by the door.

—

Jacqui has suggested I resume shorter twice-weekly appointments with Robin here at the office until the case report meeting is over and we can reformulate our plan. Rather than worry Robin by explaining that we shouldn't leave the building while her case is under review, I try to engage her in drawing a new picture when she arrives this morning.

But Robin refuses to sit down. She's used to me grabbing my coat off a hook at this point so we can go and catch the bus to the university. She leans over and puts her fingers on the table, using it as an imaginary keyboard.

"We need to do a little work here in the office today, okay? It'll be fun."

She hammers her fingers against the imaginary keys.

"I promise, we'll play the piano again soon."

At this she slumps into a seat, still wearing her coat, and begins to pick at a scab on the back of her hand.

"We haven't done any drawing in a while," I say, offering her a blue pencil crayon. When she refuses to take it, I put the pencil to the paper myself. "I just moved into a new apartment," I begin, sketching the outline of my mother's tiered building. "And I live up here on the fifth floor." I add four horizontal lines, layering the building like a cake.

"And you live with Miriam and Jack Peters."

She lifts her head at their names. "In a house?" I say, drawing the outline of a house with a peaked roof. "Or an apartment?" I say, tapping the outline of my mother's building.

"Do you have your own room?" I ask, drawing a rectangle to the side of the house. I add a window and a bed to the room.

She picks up a green pencil crayon then, scribbles out the window I have drawn and adds a second bed. She throws down the pencil and crosses her arms.

"You share a room with their daughter," I say, stating the obvious, then begin to sketch the layout of my mother's apartment. "I have two bedrooms in my new place." I add one bed to the bedroom, the other to the solarium.

Robin seems bored by this, irritated, still not forgiving me for denying her time at the piano. She scrapes her chair back, walks over to the radio and starts fiddling with the dial.

"It's just me in the apartment, I don't share it with anyone," I continue, but she's not listening. She's turned the volume down very low and has pushed her ear up against the speaker.

Feeling frustrated, I put down my pencil. She has no idea of the urgency, how little time we have to waste.

I walk over to the radio and impulsively pull the plug out of the wall behind the filing cabinet.

Robin raises her eyebrows in shock. She looks like she might hit me.

"Wait," I say, holding up my forefinger. "I have something for you."

I fetch my briefcase, putting it down on the table, and pop the latch.

"Here," I say, holding the egg out to her.

She reaches for it, cups it in both hands, then puts the smooth marble to her cheek.

"*Gamarjoba*," I whisper.

Robin slowly turns her face toward me. I have no idea how to read her expression. Have I just betrayed her trust or earned it?

"Secret," I say, bringing my finger to my lips.

"*Garmarjoba*," she whispers, secret shared.

—

On the weekend, a moving van comes for the rest of my things. I don't even take a final look around my apartment for anything that might have been left behind, I just put the key on the kitchen counter and pull the door closed behind me.

The rest of my day is spent arranging my furniture, trying to make it work in my mother's old place. I need to grow up; my stuff looks shabby, lost in all this space. I probably need a dining room table.

I order a pizza in the early evening and begin unpacking my books. I am squashing down the nagging desire to drink that always accompanies the setting of the sun. I busy myself arranging my books on the top three shelves, purging the self-help with incriminating titles and a copy of *Fifty Shades of Grey* that I bought on a whim and immediately regretted.

On the shelf below, I put our music: the compilation of beginner classics, the Liszt concerto and a volume of études. Beside our slim collection I put my father's old tape recorder and box of tapes. On the last shelf I place a selection of some favourite books from childhood, ones Robin might enjoy: an illustrated copy of *The Wizard of Oz*, some *Beezus and Ramona*s and a couple of Judy Blumes, all of which can keep her *Heidi* company.

The intercom buzzes. It's Vlad, groaning that I have a delivery. It's the bed I've ordered, but I am too exhausted to deal with it now so I have the delivery guys just bring it up and prop it to the left of the entryway. I fall asleep in my clothes soon after, too tired to get up and brush my teeth.

In the morning, I tip over the giant box in the entryway and drag it into the solarium. I slice through the cardboard with a knife and lay out all the pieces. It takes ages to put together with an Allen key and a screwdriver, but it's such a pretty bed, with a headboard constructed from two white metal swans, their necks intertwined.

I set up my computer and print out a schedule for AA meetings a reasonable distance away, nowhere too close, and nowhere I might run into someone I know. I tape it to the fridge, display it like one might a child's art, and put the empty bottles that have accumulated in the corner of the kitchen into a black plastic bag. It's got to look good in the event of a home visit. To that end, I'd better stock the cupboards.

I walk to the grocery store in the plaza. I haven't made dinner since I was with Michael, a time that feels like another life now. I'm a little overzealous with my shopping, in need of even the most basic things, and end up with far more than I can possibly carry home. I have to ask the cashier if I can leave the rest of the bags and come back for them.

"Special occasion?" she asks.

I smile and thank her, returning forty minutes later for the rest of the bags.

—

It's the day before Robin's case review and I've been up all night. I spent the early-morning hours memorizing some more basic Georgian words and phrases, mouthing them to myself on the streetcar, then throwing out the list before I got to work.

Robin looks a little sheepish when she enters my office today. She pulls a button out of her coat pocket, an ornate enamel button with a gold stripe through it, and puts it on the table before me.

"That's very beautiful," I say.

She pushes it closer to me.

"Is that for me?"

She nods.

"*Gmadlob*," I try, thanking her in an awkward crush of consonants.

"*Ara pris*," she whispers.

"What is your name?" I try in Georgian.

"Maia," she says.

I don't know how to ask for her last name.

I say the word for mother, but she shakes her head. "No mother?" I ask.

When I say the word for father, though, it is as if I have struck a match. Robin stands up abruptly and shouts: "*Ara! Ara!*"

"It's okay," I say, putting my hand on her shoulder. I am imagining the worst: years of abuse by her father. But now she is kicking my office door. I imagine it's the door to her basement room, trying to get out, get away from him, but the sound must have alerted Mirabelle, because suddenly my door is being pushed open and Mirabelle is forcing herself in.

"What's going on?" she says.

Robin grabs my hand and tugs and Mirabelle reaches out to stop her, placing her hand on my forearm. Robin shakes my arm, throwing Mirabelle's hand off roughly.

"*Tsamomkhjevit!*" she shouts.

My heart starts pounding. Mirabelle places herself between Robin and the door.

Jacqui steps out of her office then to see what the commotion is about.

It's as if a rock has just been thrown at a wall of glass and no one dares breathe, waiting to see if the glass will shatter. I am squeezing Robin's hand so hard that the beds of my nails have turned white, but I cannot seem to let go.

ADAM

EVERY FRIDAY at noon, the place clears out as the muezzin calls the faithful to *Jumu'ah* prayers. Adam wonders if he could pass for one of them now that he can touch his beard to his chest. He has had dreams of living inside someone else's body. One night it was Oskar: Adam inside Oskar's body, desperately trying not to reveal his presence by thinking his own thoughts. The residue of that dream had lingered on, revisiting him several mornings in a row, forcing him to actively relocate himself, saying *That is Oskar, this is me.*

In the however many months he has been here, there has not been any interrogation, or invitation to make a statement, or even a sighting of anyone higher up. It must be a deliberate strategy to fuck a person up.

The whole notion of time has become abstract. A day is a day like the one just before it. Five calls to prayer, three meals, four glasses of tea. They shit and piss in their designated buckets in opposite corners. Abdi takes those buckets away, empties and returns them. The call to prayer has no meaning for Adam. Without Abdi, there would be no structure to Adam's day, no civility at all.

One Friday, at the beginning of the rainy season, Oskar rises with the noon call to prayer, heading for the door. In all these months, Adam has not ventured past the threshold. He has never seen Oskar do so before, either.

"A new development," Oskar says, smug satisfaction on his face.

So I am the only unfaithful one in this house, Adam thinks— in this house, in this compound, perhaps even in this country. He feels a tightening in his chest, a surge of fear, adrenalin.

Hearing everyone clear out of the building, Adam decides to risk hobbling down the hall. He pulls himself up with effort and shuffles along the wall of the room, his palm against it. With Oskar out of the way, Adam realizes that he has been as much this man's captive as anyone's. Oskar and the kidnappers are echoes of each other, reinforcements, inner and outer walls.

When he reaches the door frame, he cranes his neck into the hall, looking to the right. He sees two doorways at the end of the bright pink, sunlit hall. He turns his head to the left, into the glare of the sun, and finds the black threat of a Kalashnikov aimed right at his face. Adam flinches as a wild-eyed boy flicks the shaft of his gun twice to the right, directing Adam back into the room. Adam withdraws his face, leaning back against the blue wall, just to the left of the door frame. He tries and fails to breathe, slithering down the wall until he is in a heap on the floor.

He sits here for some time. He catches the scent of onions and garlic frying somewhere nearby, the faint chatter of women as they cook. Then he hears the distinct sound of Abdi shuffling down the concrete hallway in his flip-flops and finds some comfort at the familiar sight of the boy in the doorway.

Abdi kneels down beside Adam on the floor. He hands Adam a blister pack of pills. Adam turns them over: expired antibiotics, from what he can make out—metronidazole. Why is Abdi doing this? Taking this kind of risk? Adam has to wonder if the boy is just as afraid of Oskar as he is of the men who have recruited him for this job, because it's only now, with Oskar out of the way, that Abdi is making this overture.

Abdi hands him a tin cup of water. "Drink," he says, bringing his thumb to his lips.

It is the first time Adam has heard him speak. "You know some English," he says.

"What is your name. I am fine, thank you," Abdi says quietly.

Adam pops a pink pill into his palm and swallows it. The antibiotics may have lost all efficacy, but this is a way to suggest he trusts the boy.

"You should be in school, not here," says Adam.

"I want Canada. Or Australia."

"You should still be in school."

"You teach me," Abdi says.

"What do you want to know?" Adam asks.

"All," Abdi replies, and Adam laughs for what feels like the first time in his life.

"Please," Abdi insists.

"Okay," says Adam. "What about numbers?"

Abdi rattles off the numbers one through ten.

"Do you know what comes next?"

Abdi shakes his head.

"So we'll start there. Eleven."

On the third round, Abdi falters at eighteen, when a baby cries and a woman shouts "Ibrahim!" The men and boys are returning from the mosque, their voices crescendoing in approach.

Abdi reaches for the blister pack and tucks it under the fabric tied around his waist.

"Thank you," Adam whispers.

"Welcome," Abdi says, disappearing with the cup of water.

Adam slides across the room on his behind, what's left of it, before the rest of them enter the house. His clothes are now hanging off him. He thinks it would be impossible to roll the waist of his jeans over one more time without castrating himself.

Oskar wears the more typical garb of an expat of his generation: beige chinos and a white—at least *once* white—button-down. The edges of his sleeves are the colour of charcoal. But when he enters their room after visiting the mosque, Adam can see they have given Oskar a change of clothes. He wears a sarong knotted at the waist and a clean white shirt. Adam thinks of a calf being fattened for slaughter and then berates himself for such potent ill-wishing.

Lunch is an extravagance, as it has been all Fridays before. A spaghetti Bolognese, surrounded by a ring of thinly sliced French fries. Adam and Oskar eat in silence from the shared platter. Then Oskar sits back and whispers: "I've brought us a little treat."

From under his *macawiis*, Oskar pulls out a piece of chocolate. Adam hears a chorus of mothers telling him not to take candy from strangers, and yet he reaches out a quivering hand.

It begins like butter on the tongue, the sweetness emerging as it melts. It is like the best of all the Halloween candy being secretly consumed under a sheet by flashlight in the middle of the night.

Oskar claims he received it as a trade for helping compose an email in English.

"To whom?" Adam asks.

"To Sofie."

Adam clenches his jaw and squeezes his hands into fists. Is Oskar fucking with him? He hates the sound of her name in this man's mouth.

"How the fuck did they find her?"

"They have their ways."

"And what was in the email?"

"The usual—a demand for ransom. They must think you're worth something; they put the price at two million."

Adam places his knuckles on the floor and starts counting to one hundred in his head.

"You miss her," Oskar says, interrupting him at fifty-five.

"Of course I fucking miss her!" Adam shouts.

"I know, I know," he says, placing his palms on the floor in front of him. "She is all you have."

You revealed too much, Adam admonishes himself. You were sick, you were weak, unguarded.

Adam remains silent, hoping to God Sofie has left the camp, that they don't know her whereabouts, that she is somewhere safe. He hopes her messages are encrypted, her ISP is masked, and that she has the State Department and some security behind her.

"Take my advice," Oskar says after a few minutes of silence. "Tell Sofie to give them what they are asking for."

"Are you kidding? Where the fuck is a pediatric nurse in Africa going to get two million dollars?"

"She will figure it out. People do."

The moon is full tonight, latticework patterning the concrete floor. Adam turns to the wall, wanting to imagine Sofie secure within the US embassy in Addis, enclosed by iron fencing, concrete, glass. He wants to picture some safe subterranean war room, crowded with men and women and machines, a complex diagram on the wall identifying potential names of his captors and a map punctuated with pins narrowing down his possible whereabouts. Circles within circles, homing in.

Oskar's breathing, thick, forced through his nostrils, is keeping him awake. Adam hopes he is dreaming of being eaten alive. But no—Oskar is not asleep at all: he is on all fours exerting himself, pushing himself against something, someone.

Adam turns back to the wall. He's nauseous, but at the same time, he feels himself growing hard. A wave of bile ripples through him and he retches; thick sorghum porridge rolling out of his mouth onto his cheek, the blanket, the floor. He lies there in that mess, pressing one ear into the floor, mashing his palm against the other, trying to block out the sound. It ends quickly with a short, explosive *pah*.

Adam wants to cry. A swish of fabric, and Abdi slides out of the room.

In the morning, Adam is once again overtaken by nausea. He retches again, the waves undulating and so forceful that he can feel liquid seeping out of his behind at the same time. He is breaking down, his body expelling all of its fluids. How long before he disintegrates altogether?

He turns his head away from Abdi when he enters the room with breakfast and again when the boy returns to mop up Adam's vomit. He avoids looking at Abdi all week. But at noon on Friday, just after Oskar leaves for the mosque, Abdi appears in the doorway again with a tin cup of water and the blister pack of pills.

This time, Abdi sits down beside him. Adam sees the soles of the boy's feet, rippled with lacerations, yet to form scars. He's afraid for Abdi, a boy evidently tortured by who knows how many of the men here. He cringes at the thought of Oskar's particular cruelty. The twisted sadism of that night hangs in the space between them and Adam worries that perhaps Oskar had sniffed some change in the air between them, sensed some communication had taken place, and that is why Abdi had been punished in this particular way, sodomized in Adam's presence: Oskar's way of asserting ownership and degrading them both.

Something inside Adam breaks. He starts to sob and Abdi scooches back in alarm.

Stop, Adam tells himself, bowing his head and taking a deep breath. He needs you to be a man—a good one.

"I'm sorry," Adam says, wiping his face on his sleeve and coughing weakly. He takes the blister pack and pops a pill directly into his mouth, swallowing it with effort.

"English," he says. "You wanted me to teach you some more English."

Abdi inches closer.

What to teach him today? Adam asks himself.

Relatives, he thinks—isn't that what we learn after basic greetings and numbers? But the boy is an orphan. And so is he. Adam casts his eyes about the room and decides on something more innocuous. He'll teach him the English for the colours they can see before them right now. The only problem is, Adam is having trouble finding the words.

—

The light has changed, brought back colour. The end of the rainy season. Perhaps they prefer a more illuminated backdrop for their videos, Adam thinks, because apparently this is the day. A young man, masked apart from his eyes, orders Adam up with a jerk of the barrel of his rifle immediately after morning prayers.

"Oh, look," says Oskar, sitting in the lotus position like some smug, aging hippie with that irritating wry smile on his face, "Faisal is here to escort you to your fifteen minutes of fame."

But first they must ensure Adam's ignominy by binding him at the wrists and ankles. Abdi does this work, kneeling on the ground at his feet, the masked man barking orders. Abdi keeps his face turned away from Adam's bad foot.

Once Abdi has finished the job, Faisal nudges Adam forward, the muzzle of his rifle in the small of his back. Adam has to lean his shoulder into the wall in order to propel himself down the pink hallway.

At the end of the hall, he stumbles over the threshold of the front room, toppling forward without his hands to break his fall. He turns his face away from the floor and feels his cheekbone crack with the impact. Four men, smoking and drinking tea as they recline against satin pillows, erupt into laughter. A fifth man, leaning against the sill of a barred window, remains stony-faced, and shouts a torrent at the young man behind Adam. Faisal leaps forward to help Adam upright. He leads Adam gingerly by the elbow to a solitary chair on the opposite side of the room.

The harsh light of the day fills the room. Adam can barely make out the men's features from where he sits facing the window. The cigarette smoke is so thick it burns his nostrils. He can feel blood crawling down his left cheek. His whole body is a heartbeat. The man standing against the windowsill considers him, staring straight ahead and stroking his beard. This must be the Mullah. Adam avoids his scrutiny, looking over his shoulder to the courtyard outside. A woman shrouded in a black abaya passes. A goat bleats.

"You will state the date, your name and the name of your country," the man says in a voice of calm velvet. "You will demand two million dollars to secure your release. You will say, 'Nothing short of this is possible.' And you will tell the US it must stop its support of the illegitimate government of Somalia."

He is well-educated and speaks fluent English with formality. Why would a man like this need any help from Oskar to compose an email in English?

"Your final statement shall be, 'If these conditions are not met, I will be promptly executed,'" the Mullah continues. "Understood? Nothing more, nothing less."

Adam nods slowly and a drop of blood falls from his chin onto his lap.

"You may take a moment to rehearse," he says, with a magnanimous wave of his hand. He crosses his arms and turns his back to Adam, staring out the window.

"I'm sorry," Adam says. "But what's the date?"

"January. January 4th," the Mullah says over his shoulder.

"What year?"

The Mullah smirks. "2009."

Adam tries to calculate how long this means he has been here, but it requires the math of another world, not this one;

and why, in any case, should he believe the Mullah, who may well be forward- or backward-dating this video to suit his purposes?

Adam goes over the lines in his head. One of the Mullah's henchmen rises and fetches a video camera on a tripod from the corner of the room. He positions it to face Adam and indicates that he should turn his head slightly so that his bloody cheek is visible. He turns the camera on, a bright glare of light flooding Adam's face, and directs Faisal to adjust the positioning of the framed Qur'anic quote behind Adam's head.

The Mullah pivots around to face Adam. "On the count of three, you may begin," he says, raising his hand in the air. Adam watches his fingers: one, two and then three of them, and the tape begins to roll.

Adam clears his throat. "My name is Daniel Rainier," he says, a tremor evident through the words.

"Stop!" shouts the Mullah so loudly that the rest of his henchmen suddenly sit up straight. He snaps his fingers and shouts an order at Faisal. Faisal rushes to stand behind Adam and puts the muzzle of his rifle just behind and above Adam's ear. "Perhaps this will help you think more clearly," says the Mullah.

"And again on the count of three," he says, raising his hand.

Adam releases his name into the wild.

Laying his cheek against the cool concrete of the floor dulls the throbbing to some extent. It also goes some way toward muffling Oskar's prattle. He's badgering Adam, wanting to know what

Adam thought of the Mullah, how many others were in the room, how he thinks Sofie will react to the video, where he thinks she might be when she first sees it. But Adam is not talking to him about Sofie. He is not talking to him about anything. Adam wonders why they have them in the same room together—wouldn't isolation make them each more desperate, more willing?

He has to start thinking like them. If you were a kidnapper, what advantage would there be to having two captives in a room? They could police each other, compelling each other to behave. They could play off each other to their own advantage—if one were to report on the other, he might gain favour with the captors. Is that what Oskar is up to? Is that why they let him attend the mosque and have given him new clothes? If so, what is he conveying to them? And what might Adam be able to reveal about him?

He has this in mind when Oskar leaves for the mosque again on Friday. Oskar has a small pile of things in his corner of the room—a pillow, a Qur'an and his old clothes. Adam scoots across the floor on his butt and gingerly begins looking for the labels. His chinos are generic Gap. His shirt is from John Lewis. And his boxers are just embarrassing—Thomas the Tank Engine, Korean-made, a gift, perhaps, from his twenty-six-year-old girlfriend.

There's something in one of the pockets of his chinos, wrapped in silver foil. More chocolate. Adam flips open Oskar's green leather-bound Qur'an to where it is bookmarked. The bookmark is from an Arabic bookstore in Paris. Arabic fills the pages, a script unintelligible to him. He has envied the ease with which many of his former European colleagues seem to pick up local languages, but to be able to read in such a different script must take years. How has Oskar developed this kind of proficiency?

Today Abdi sees Adam over by Oskar's things and shakes his head, looking worried. He comes into the room and kneels down beside Adam, placing the tin cup in Adam's hands. Abdi sets about carefully restacking Oskar's clothes.

"He is bad man," Abdi whispers.

Adam points to the window. He mimes the action of sawing through the lattice.

Abdi shakes his head.

Adam shrugs his shoulders and raises his palms.

Abdi raises an imaginary knife to his throat.

Oskar returns for lunch, but Adam has lost his appetite. He can no longer even stand the sound of the Norwegian swallowing. When he is finished eating, Oskar wipes his fleshy lips on the back of his hand, then asks: "Did you find what you were looking for?"

Adam can feel his face burning.

"You know what they do with a thief here, don't you? You better be a bit more careful. You and your little friend."

"I was looking for chocolate. Abdi had nothing to do with it."

Oskar scoffs, then starts cleaning his nails with his teeth. "Oh, by the way," he says a moment later, spitting something onto the floor. "I heard the men chatting on the way back.

Apparently they've heard from your Sofie."

"What? What were they saying?"

"I wasn't really close enough to catch the rest."

"Oh, come on!" Adam shouts.

"All I made out was 'one million.'"

"She's offered them a million or they've lowered the ransom by a million?"

Oskar shrugs. "I couldn't say."

"Jesus Christ!" Adam shouts. "Stop being such a fucking bastard!"

"Danny, Danny," he says, putting his hand on Adam's shoulder. "You should be thanking me. I am the only reason you are still alive."

"What do you mean?"

"They didn't want the complication of you," he says. "They brought you here to kill you. But I stepped in and told them you were much more valuable to them alive than dead. They could get themselves two million dollars for an American."

"Wait," Adam says, waving his hand at Oskar's face. "Stop." He is trying but failing to put this together in his head. He brokered a deal with them? For what reason? To secure his own freedom?

"Why didn't you just let them kill me?" Adam finally says.

Oskar smiles in that greasy way of his.

"Come on," Adam persists. "It wasn't for the company."

Nothing. He's giving Adam nothing but a shrug. "Please. Could you stop fucking with my head?" Adam shouts and feels winded by the effort, breathless.

The noise brings Faisal and one of the Mullah's henchmen scuttling down the hall to their door.

Oskar says something in Arabic to them over his shoulder. To Adam, he says: "My work here is done." He runs a long look of hate down the entire length of Adam's body. "Oh, and you might want to ask for the butcher," he says, nodding at Adam's foot.

—

Abdi arrives with Adam's breakfast the next morning, placing the tray down, avoiding his eyes. He goes to the other side of the room then to collect Oskar's things. Adam wonders if the boy has been reprimanded, beaten, why he is not speaking to him. He watches him silently place a small pile of folded clothes onto the prayer rug along with Oskar's Qur'an. Abdi rolls up the rug, clutches it under one arm, and leaves the room as if he's just dismantled a set between scenes.

Adam stares at the spot where Oskar's things used to be, wondering how it is possible that all trace of this man could vanish in under a minute. There is nothing to suggest he was ever here.

He stares at the tray, with its porridge and tea, and the floor tilts, bringing a wave of nausea that forces Adam to lie down. The concrete, feeling clammy against his cheek, smells like urine, as if Oskar has marked the place like a dog.

When Abdi comes for his tray later, he kneels down in front of Adam and looks at him intently. Abdi raises his hand to his mouth, mimes eating.

Adam shakes his head and mutters: "Can't."

"Drink," says Abdi. Adam attempts to push himself upright. Feeling weak and dizzy, he leans against the wall, letting his head fall back.

"Open," says Abdi, with a teaspoon at Adam's lips. Adam might be wrong, but it looks like Abdi has lost his front teeth. Adam opens his own mouth. Abdi slides in a spoonful of honey. "Make strong," he says, pointing to the window.

Adam draws an imaginary knife across his neck.

Abdi shakes his head.

Make strong, Adam repeats in his mind, strong enough to hoist the boy onto your shoulders and escape.

What Adam notices first when he next wakes is the silence. The quiet he has become accustomed to is a low and incessant hum—dulled voices in a far-off room, the occasional reprimanding cry of a woman, the Mullah's engine, the slosh of a bucket being emptied, the bleating of goats and the chatter of chickens. But today there is no sound, none at all until the call to prayer, as if a bomb exploded in the night, killing off everyone but him and the muezzin.

"Abdi?" Adam calls out weakly.

Abdi appears in the door frame a minute later, his eyes beseeching.

"Where is everyone?" Adam asks.

Abdi issues a torrent of words in Somali, and Adam notices the rifle at his side.

"What's going on?" Adam asks. He tries, but doesn't have the strength to stand up. He crawls over to the doorway to look down the hall. He sees no one, but can now hear the purr of a well-oiled engine outside.

Someone kicks open the door at the end of the hall just then and the outline of a giant fills the frame. Abdi tugs at Adam's good leg, trying to drag him back into the room. Adam inches backward like a caterpillar in reverse, cursing. He tries to push himself upright, pressing his palms into the floor. Abdi finishes the job, yanking him up by the shirt and leaning his slight frame against Adam's back, propping him up as best as he can while shaking.

The giant moves with such stealth that Adam sees the thick tip of some military-grade weapon round the corner of the door frame before he hears so much as a footstep. A huge white man of indeterminate nationality slinks into view, his flak jacket unadorned with the emblem or insignia of any army, his weapon raised, ammunition strapped to his legs.

Adam silently begs Abdi not to do anything stupid with the rifle. He raises his own hands in surrender, hoping Abdi will do the same. "There's no threat here," he says. "The ones you want have left."

The giant takes aim. The shot is as quiet as a stapler. Abdi emits something guttural behind Adam, shooting his rifle at the ceiling as he falls backwards. With Abdi's weight no longer against his back, Adam slumps backwards as well, his head landing on Abdi's spasming thighs.

"Fuck!" Adam shouts at the ceiling. "You just shot a kid, why would you shoot a kid?"

There are two giant white men in the room now: private contractors obviously hired to get him out.

Adam gropes for Abdi's hand, wanting to check for a pulse even though he knows it's futile.

"He was just a child," Adam says, staring at his own now-bloodied hand.

The first man reaches down then and swiftly scoops Adam up under the arms like he's a toddler, folding him over his shoulder in a fireman's lift.

"You can't just leave him there," says Adam, staring at the pool of dark blood spreading out from underneath Abdi's head.

In less than a minute, Adam has been transferred into an armoured, air-conditioned vehicle. They tear away in a cloud of dust, Adam's head bobbing against the back seat. A meaty hand passes him a bottle of water over the headrest. "The fewer questions asked, the better," its owner says in an eastern European accent.

On the Ethiopian side of the border, they pick up a doctor who checks Adam's vitals, props up his feet, secures a mask connected to a portable oxygen tank over his mouth, palpates his inner elbow in search of a good vein, inserts a needle attached to a catheter and hangs three bags of clear liquid from the coat hook above the window to feed and medicate him intravenously.

"You should be dead," the doctor says, and Adam thinks: Yes. I should be dead.

—

Adam has dreams about running across desert, getting no-where, sinking in sand amongst carcasses in various stages of decay, a vast graveyard under the sun. Each time he wakes up he is seized with the quiet terror of not knowing where he is. He takes in the white sheets, the bed, the various tubes spider-ing out of the bruised underside of his arm and the beeping of a heart monitor, and he wonders if he has been in a car acci-dent. His foot will twitch, as if he is searching for a brake, but then he will remember that he doesn't have that foot anymore.

They amputated his leg below the knee within hours of his arrival at the hospital in Addis Ababa. A BKA, they call it. They also took a kidney. Adam has not wanted to look down, but he has wanted to run.

Sofie is here, offering him water to clear away the sand that has accumulated between his teeth in his dreams. He can see his admission date on a chart on the wall, but can recall little about the last two weeks. It's as if his mind and body have become detached from each other. He will suddenly become aware of Sofie holding his hand, stroking his forehead, repeating some-thing that he has just heard in his head, her voice a confusing echo. He touches his lips, certain that he has not spoken aloud.

It is only now that he can take Sofie in. She has weathered in the eight months since he last saw her; grey has gathered at her temples and the slight indentation between her eyebrows that used to appear when she was worried now has a place in every expression. He sees a look of imploring and he knows he is not up to whatever she wants from him—not now, perhaps not ever.

"I am sorry," is all he can think to say.

In general, Adam nods and says what he thinks are the right words into the bleed of open mouths before him. Whatever he says is without any particular feeling, without the obvious gratitude and relief he imagines a person in this position would or should or might show. An outpouring like that probably requires feeling like a person, which he doesn't, not exactly.

While he can speak now, his thoughts are not in the room. The one thought consuming his energy and attention is that had those mercenaries come just one day earlier, they would have found Oskar in that room. It would have been Oskar lying dead in a pool of his own blood then, not Abdi, and Adam would have found some relief in that, perhaps even pleasure, rather than the guilt that haunts him now.

"Adam, who is Oskar?" Sofie asks one morning when he wakes up.

She is calling him Adam now, whoever is in the room. Is he Adam now? Is Daniel Rainier dead?

"It's complicated," Adam says.

"It's okay," she says. "Save your energy."

Because there will be plenty of talking in his near future, Adam knows. He is a man who has just cost his government two million dollars. There will be an extensive debriefing—standard operating procedure—with consular staff here and in Nairobi and with the State Department in Washington. Adam will have to tell the whole story over and over in detail and provide an intelligence report with names and physical descriptions. He'll be asked to scrutinize maps, photos, grainy video footage, composite sketches. And he will tell them about the mysterious Oskar, try to enlist their help in figuring out his role in all this.

After breakfast this morning, Sofie takes a taxi over to the Hilton to check email and Titune comes to lead him through half an hour of exercises. She's very pretty, a young Harari woman with freckles across her nose who trained as a physiotherapist in Dubai. She uncovers Adam's legs and helps him swing them over the side of the bed. His stump is wrapped tightly in order to reduce the swelling. In about three months he'll be fitted with a temporary prosthesis.

While Titune has him doing leg lifts, Adam asks her questions, coming alive with the possibility of talking about anything other than being here. He's always meant to visit Harar, but has never managed to find the opportunity. The walled city has a reputation as a mysterious and holy place, the Hararis protective and proud of it though allegedly not particularly welcoming to outsiders. He has heard that they feed the hyenas who roam the nearby hills.

"Is it a religious tradition?" he asks her this morning.

"This drama with the hyena man? This is a show for the tourists. But the hyenas are coming at night to eat the garbage so we must treat them with respect. Once a year some sheikhs in the hills make a ritual and give them porridge. It is a cultural practice, not a religious one."

She taps his leg lightly. "Concentrate, Mr. Adam. Straighten from the knee." Adam again—he is Adam to everyone here.

"Are the lines between religion and culture always that clear?" he asks.

She stands back to consider this for a moment. "They become clear with literacy," she says. "Are you interested in our religion, Mr. Adam?"

He can only shrug. He is not interested in the sense in which she is asking. Adam finds it hard to relate to the idea of being anchored by or bound to any set of beliefs. He can see the appeal of having a comprehensive way of seeing the world, a systematic way of relating to it. But the fervour he has seen, that is something else.

"I will pray for you," she says.

"I don't know if it will do any good."

"Keep your heart open, Mr. Adam. You have suffered a great injury. Your leg will be okay with support. Perhaps your heart needs some support too."

And with that slightly preachy but strangely touching piece of advice, Titune is gone for the day.

—

Sofie returns with copies of the *Herald Tribune* and the *Financial Times*. She's also printed out a stack of emails she wants him to read. But Adam can't focus on text. Reading a newspaper is like looking through a dirty window. He shakes his head at her offer of the *Times*.

"You might want to read this email at least," she says, holding out a sheet of paper.

But the effort it would require seems overwhelming. Adam leans his head back. "Maybe you could just read it to me," he says, closing his eyes.

His eyelids feel like they're made out of lead. He can feel a tingling in his stump, as if his foot is falling asleep. He wishes he could turn over, not have to sleep on his back, but the confusion of wires prevents it. Sofie is silent. Adam pries open his eyelids with his fingers. She is sitting on the end of his bed with her forehead in her hands, crying.

"Sofie," he says, trying to muster some compassion. It's not that he feels unkind, exactly, but he does feel irritated and exhausted.

She wipes her eyes with her sleeve. "It's okay, Adam," she says. "It's just . . . just a lot."

He closes his eyes. In her presence, he is weighed down by the awareness of his failure to feel and express gratitude. But he doesn't think he can bear the burden of having been saved, not at the cost of seeing the only glimmer of innocence and kindness in that fucked up world extinguished.

The Mullah and his men left Abdi behind in order to punish him. For being Adam's "little friend," in Oskar's words: a traitor.

But the contractors just took him out—the enemy, collateral damage. Perhaps it is naïve of him to believe that US soldiers would have been forced to use more restraint, but those thugs are not accountable to any government.

"Why did they send private contractors, not US soldiers, to get me out?" Adam asks Sofie.

"I don't know all the details, Adam, but does it matter who got you out? You're alive, isn't that what matters?"

Adam stares out the window at the grey sky.

It is grey in Addis for months at a time. It's an ugly mash-up of a city, most African capitals are: remnants from colonial days mixed with the brutalist architecture of dictatorships interwoven with the sprawling makeshift housing of the impoverished majority, nowhere left uninhabited, garbage dumps and cemeteries becoming cities unto themselves. The way most of the world lives is just shit.

The next time he sees Titune, she has a gift for him, a Qur'an with the Arabic verses on the right side of each page, their English translations on the left. "It will give you no spiritual benefit to read in English, but maybe it will give you some understanding," she says.

Some, but not enough. He berates himself for ever having excused himself from learning the language, for thinking of this lack as little more than a disadvantage and an inconvenience, for his reliance on translators, for behaving more like an expat than an expert.

In captivity he was a victim of his own limitations, forced to rely for information on the least reliable of humans simply because Oskar spoke a language that he did not. What lies was Oskar feeding him? What critical information passed right over his head? What would he, could he, have picked up that would have allowed him to play the whole situation differently?

His arrogance and impatience have cost him. There has always been the option to take a six-month intensive language course at the Defense Language Institute, fully paid for by the State Department. And he has never even considered it. Not until now.

"I'm going to read this in Arabic one day," he tells Titune.

"Inshallah," she says, smiling, the lines around her eyes suggesting she is older than he thought, a married woman, a mother.

Sofie reacts somewhat differently to the idea when he later tells her.

"If you're having fantasies of heading off to Iraq—" she says, her frustration evident, "—Adam—I thought we could focus on building something of a life for ourselves in the US—you know, a home."

"It's a nod to your heritage," he says.

She swallows hard, uncertain. He is lying, they both know that. But she is trying her best to believe otherwise.

TESS

IT'S HARD to say when I fell out of love. I'd only been in love, if I can call it that, once before. As a graduate student at Yale, I'd had a very painful obsession with a professor, something I tried to work out of my system by going to New York every weekend and having sex with random women I met in bars. Eventually, I didn't have time to go to New York: the pressure to finish my thesis, to publish in the right peer-reviewed journals, to find a permanent job, to put out a book and work toward tenure left no room for much beyond the occasional ill-advised hookup at a conference.

And then Emily. I found it unnerving at first to have someone gaze back at me with a particular softness in her eyes that left her open and invited me in. I would ask Emily sometimes, What makes you so certain?

"I just know," she would say.

"Do we know or do we make a decision?"

"That's probably a chicken-and-egg question."

I asked the same question of myself five years later when I began to think of leaving. Did I know or was I making a decision? It had been a process of erosion that resulted in a decision, the exact moment of my departure just one moment in an accumulation of the many that were piling up in my chest until I couldn't breathe.

I tolerated, at best, the rituals of dealing with a newborn. Emily had instincts I didn't. I loathed my unfamiliar body and counted the weeks to the start of the fall term.

With me gone, Emily got busy making friends, doing Mom-and-Me swimming/singing/yoga, and joining a mothers' group. I have to confess I was completely uninterested. All that quiet competition between mothers over head circumferences and cruising and teeth. The failure-to-breastfeed stories in which Emily found such comfort. She had spent a painful and frustrating month trying to produce milk herself, taking herbal supplements, then pills, and attaching a breast pump, without much success.

I went to the mothers' group at her insistence a total of once. The women struck me as interchangeable, with their expensive jogging strollers and Lululemon leggings and blonde highlights in need of touching up. And they seemed so young, like girls playing at being mothers. I could not have felt more alien.

They met on Monday and Thursday mornings at a park close to our house. The babies who were awake were plonked onto a communal blanket for all-important tummy time.

One of the women asked Emily for the name of the medication she'd taken when she was trying to breastfeed.

"Something that began with a D," she said, "but I really didn't have much luck with it."

"My sister is really beating herself up about not being able to breastfeed," the woman said.

"Oh my God," said one of the other women. "Tell her to steer clear of lactation consultants. Total Nazis."

Emily had two of these women over on a wintry morning a couple of months later. Out came the communal blanket, and once the babies were wrangled out of Snuglis and snowsuits and rolling around, I could see how inevitable it was that mothers made comparisons.

I was bringing in a tray of coffee when I commented that it was hard to imagine how Max had fit inside me with those feet.

"Oh," said one of the women, glancing over at Emily. "I always assumed you were the biological mom."

Emily just shrugged. We agreed that the question of which one of us was the biological mother was an intrusive and offensive one, irrelevant, nobody's business, too privileging of nature over nurture, and yet coming up against these assumptions in reality bothered me in some fundamental way.

Emily later accused me of deliberately trying to assert myself as the "real" mother. She went as far as calling it an act of betrayal. She wasn't entirely wrong. She was doing the bulk of the work, she was the one these women saw with our baby day-to-day, and yet I wanted to be recognized for my role in this.

I resented the assumption that mother and motherhood had to look a certain way.

A day later, both us having softened, she said: "We need to be a team. A united front." We were at this pub we used to love, where she had a martini and I had a pint, and she was telling me about this woman she'd met in yoga, a single mother, a new friend.

"We compared ID numbers," Emily had said, laughing.

"You what?"

"Donor IDs. Just in case they're diblings."

I didn't think there was anything funny about this—and *diblings*? "Can we not use that word?" I said.

"Whatever. Half-siblings, then. Chances are he has some. Aren't you curious?"

"It doesn't matter if I'm curious or not. I think that's Max's business, not ours. If it's something he wants to seek out when he's older, of course I'd support him, but at this point?"

"It doesn't mean we couldn't find out. You don't think it could be nice for him to know he has that kind of extended family?"

"Family?" I said. "We're his family, Emily. He has plenty of family—aunts, uncles, cousins, a grandfather—"

"—your family."

"Our family."

I felt protective of my father in that moment. He'd privately wrestled with his Catholicism, worked hard at it, and he'd embraced Emily, us. His affection for her was genuine. She seemed to be looking for something more, though, something she felt was closer to her, perhaps: a sense of family that came through our child, rather than through me.

I might have had no instinct for babies, but I definitely had an instinct for the boy Max became. As he got older, what I looked forward to, what I relished increasingly, was my time alone with him. On the weekends, when Emily wanted to catch up on sleep, I'd take him to soccer, swimming, movies, wrestle with him, spend hours in the park, make up treasure hunts and games. When it was warm enough we sometimes set up a tent in the backyard and slept out there together. We would skewer marshmallows and heat them over a candle. We would count the stars as they appeared until there were just too many to count.

When we were snuggled into our sleeping bags and the world was silent except for the occasional whoosh of a vehicle, the metal squeal of an old garage door opening in the laneway, or raccoons lunging into garbage bins, he would sometimes ask me questions about where he came from.

Max has never not known he was conceived with the help of a donor, but his questions about what this means have evolved over time. I try to keep the answers as simple and honest as possible, not giving him more than he is asking for, assuming he is asking for what he can handle knowing.

At first the questions concerned his conception. I explained that a baby was made by putting an egg together with some sperm and mixing them up. Later, he wanted to know where the egg and sperm had come from. I told him the egg had come from me and the sperm had come from a donor, a man who'd wanted to help people have children, and that the mixing had taken place at a doctor's office. Eventually he wanted to know how all that had ended up in my stomach.

He once asked me the donor's name.

"We don't know his name, buddy," I said.

"That's not fair," he said, because at his age everything was not fair.

When Max was about to start kindergarten, Emily told me she'd decided not to go back to work, saying the hours in TV just weren't compatible with motherhood. You don't know that yet, I wanted to say, and if that does prove to be true, why not find another role to play in this industry you once had such ambition and appetite for, a role that can satisfy that side of you—because there is still that side of you, isn't there?

She was thinking of going back to school and doing an MA in film preservation instead. I could feel my resentment turning into contempt. I hated the feeling, the worst of all feelings, a rot that sets in and only grows.

I didn't know what to do. I called my father in Florida, probably looking for his permission. I told him Emily and I had grown apart, we were less of a couple, a family, than we were two parents who shared a child. We were living separately in the same space; it was time to give each other the freedom to live independently of each other, is how I put it.

"You have kids with someone, you're gonna be dealing with them for the rest of your life, whether you want to or not," he said in his Greek-inflected English. "Believe me."

When my mother was diagnosed with severe anxiety and depression my father had relieved her of all duties as a wife and mother. He'd protected us from her as much as he could, renting her a separate apartment. He supported her for the rest of her life, not only paying her rent, but making sure she had groceries, and helping her transition in and out of hospital five or six times over the next couple of decades. He kept us away from all that.

My mother wouldn't have survived without my father looking after her—he must have known that.

"This is a very different situation," I said to my dad.

"How come you're always telling me I gotta view it as just the same, then? I had to get my head around the idea that Emily was just as much a mother as you are. There was a time you didn't talk to me for months because I was struggling with that idea, you remember? But I got there. You made me."

In the New Year, I started looking for an apartment nearby. It was only once I'd signed a lease that I told Emily I wasn't happy and was going to move out. I know it was the coward's way.

Emily exploded. "How can you do this? Without even trying to work on the relationship? Without any discussion? You never talk, Tess. I always have to guess how you're feeling—I mean fuck, do you even know? Do you even understand what you're doing? You're about to destroy our life, Max's world."

I'd be two blocks away, I assured her, I'd carry on paying the mortgage; not all that much would have to change in Max's world. We were already largely living separate lives as it was.

"You are so fucking cold," she managed, before she broke down completely.

My father is still the person I call. He's the only person I really talk to. When I wake from a restless night back home in my own bed, I call him in Florida to tell him about our time in Plaka. When my mother died a few years ago, he moved down to Orlando to be with my sister Carla and her husband. He has his own adjacent suite of rooms in their condo: living room, bedroom, bathroom, a balcony through a sliding glass door with an uninspiring view over a multi-lane highway lined with identical buildings. Max loves the pool in the complex, half indoors, half out, and the fact that his pappouli keeps a freezer stuffed with popsicles and ice cream.

When I reach my father, he's having his morning Nespresso out on the balcony. Carla bought him a machine for his birthday and he's religious about using it. It must have rained in the night; I can hear the slosh of cars passing below.

He's seen the photos I sent to Carla by email and he's telling me how much seeing Max in Plaka reminds him of when he was a boy. He suddenly stops his reminiscing, though, and asks, "What's the matter, Teresa?"

"It's Emily," I say. "She wants to have another child."

"Ahh," he says.

"She wants to use the remaining embryos."

He pauses for a moment and says somewhat tentatively: "You used to talk about maybe giving Max a sibling."

"That was a long time ago. A different life, you know?"

"I get it, Teresa. It's like she's going ahead with the old plans."

"We're not that family anymore."

"I gotta ask you, Teresa: Why'd you keep the embryos?"

"I didn't really think about it, Dad. We were busy. The storage fee just came out of my account automatically once a year. I didn't even notice it."

"I wonder how Max would feel about a brother or sister at this point."

"He's never mentioned wanting a sibling. Not at any point. Not once."

What Max would say when he was younger, was that he wished he had a dad. "Every family is different in its own way," I would tell him.

I once heard Emily tell Max that she had known in her gut that our donor was the one who was meant to be the father of our children. I took issue with her referring to him as a father and to imbuing our choice, which had been a practical one, with some kind of deeper significance. Why create longing for something he will never have, a fantasy about someone he will never know?

The last time he'd asked anything about his donor he'd been wondering about his interests. Did his donor play soccer and like fishing and did he know how to play chess?

I tried to explain that how you grow up, your environment, has everything to do with who you become, what choices are available to you, but he wasn't satisfied with that as an answer. So I told Max what I knew from the donor's profile: he was intelligent, had an aptitude for math and liked to play baseball. He also looked a little bit like Emily.

The sperm bank we'd used had a matching program. We'd scanned and emailed photos of Emily at different ages and in return, received three profiles of donors with the greatest physical likeness to her. Apart from sharing her colouring, Max is some combination of the Iriotakises and a man we don't know. As a sibling would be.

"Dad, you do realize that if Emily uses those embryos, she would be giving birth to your grandchild?"

"Well, that would make me a very happy pappouli."

My heart sinks. He's supposed to be on my side, my team. I don't want to go through this again. Those early years are gruelling. But now Max is at a beautiful age, becoming himself. He is enough, so much more than enough.

—

The waiting room at Solomon Feldstein LLB is expensive, with a white marble floor and tasteful light-grey linen-papered walls, two Burtynsky photos of salt mines in Rajasthan hanging above a white leather couch I'm almost afraid to sit on. The view south runs all the way down Bay Street to the lake. This man charges $675 per hour.

"Mr. Feldstein will see you now," says the receptionist. She's perfected some way of walking on her toes so you don't hear the clickety-clack of her heels. That can't be comfortable.

Stepping into Mr. Feldstein's office is like walking into a DA's office in the 1950s, completely at odds with the uber-modern boutique-hotel-lobby feel out there.

He is also something from an earlier era, in his bow tie and suspenders.

"Call me Solomon," he says, pushing himself up from a wooden desk stacked high with case files and research papers and reaching across the chaos in order to shake my hand. The whole office is a mess: paper and books spilling from shelves and law journals stacked up so high on the window ledge that they partially block the expensive view.

I take a seat in a lumpy brown leather chair, the arm stained by white coffee-cup rings. The walls in the office are a kind of brown that hasn't been seen since 1975. "You could be accused of false advertising," I say.

He laughs. "I sold the business two years ago. New guys wanted to modernize. I said do whatever you want, just don't touch my office. So," he leans forward, folding his hands on his desk. "How can I help, Dr. Iriotakis?"

"All I'm looking for at this point is a quick consultation."

"That's what they all say."

I outline the situation for him. Broad, simple strokes. I'm determined to keep this under fifteen minutes: $168.75. Plus HST.

"This whole area of assisted reproduction is an evolving area within the law, as I'm sure you can appreciate, Dr. Iriotakis.

As of yet, there is no statutory or case law for us to reference in a situation like this."

"None? Not even with a straight couple?"

"Not in Canada."

"What about in the US?"

"A handful of cases where both parties have a genetic connection to the material, but there's been very little consistency in terms of argument or judgment. It very much depends on the state—you end up in debates about when personhood begins and whether an embryo has a right to life. Even in a more rational landscape you get the argument that embryos are not merely property in the way of other assets to be divided, which lands you in this sticky area where the embryo is not quite property but is not quite a person either."

"So what is it, then?"

He shrugs his shoulders, palms up. "Depends who you are, where you are, and what you want it to be."

I slump back in the big brown leather chair, the kind that will swallow you up if you don't resist it. I stare at my shoes. Even the carpet is brown.

"Now," he says, leaning forward, "presumably you had some kind of agreement regarding disposal of the embryos in the event of a divorce or death. Most clinics oblige their patients to sign some kind of consent form about this now—or at least they should."

"We signed a bunch of things," I say, shaking my head.

"Without counsel. You see, this is the problem with these contracts, one of many problems, not the least of which being life moves on and people change their minds. You might want to find out what preferences you indicated first—then, if you care to come back and tell me what you've discovered, I'll waive the fee for today," he says.

"I appreciate it," I say, standing up and shaking his hand.

It's a Tuesday night, the night I take Max to swimming lessons. He can really motor through the water after all the swimming this summer, but his technique has grown a little wild.

"It's really different from swimming in the ocean, isn't it?" I say, glancing at my boy in the rear-view mirror on our way home. His hair is matted from his refusal to take a shower after his lesson, and he's got chocolate all over his chin. I gesture at him in the mirror: "Ice cream, right here."

His tongue is failing him. When I stop outside the house, I lean back and smear his face with my thumb. "Let's erase the evidence," I say.

I follow Max up the walkway to the house. I used to prune the bushes and the lilac tree out here, while Emily did the flowers. The bushes are looking overgrown and unruly and it appears I didn't do as good a job as I hoped with the paving stones; some of them are beginning to subside.

Max does his secret knock on the door. Emily swings open the door and swallows him up in an embrace. "You didn't have a shower, did you? Come on, let's get you in the bath," she says, patting Max's butt and encouraging him up the stairs.

"We should chat," she says to me. "I'll just go start his bath."

I make my way to the kitchen and plug in the kettle. I always experience a flicker of confusion when I'm back here. We decided not to sell the house until Max graduates from high school so that he has the continuity of a childhood home. The house is showing some signs of neglect, but nothing really changes apart from the pictures on the fridge.

Emily comes back down and sits across from me at the kitchen counter. Her grey is really coming in.

I find myself looking down at the counter, tracing my finger over the ring of a pot that had been burned into the wood surface at one of our more raucous dinner parties, before we had Max. Evidence of our former life.

"You've been very silent on the subject of my news," she says.

"I honestly don't understand why you would even want to have a child at this point. You just started a new job."

"With a very generous maternity leave. I want a family, Tess. I love being a mother. I'd like the experience of carrying a child myself. I always have."

"What about the endometriosis?"

"I had it dealt with."

When did that happen?

"Look, I'm going to need you to sign this form," she says, reaching for an envelope and sliding it across the counter.

I stare at her for a minute, then look down at my boots. The floor seems to undulate a bit. Her body, her needs. They have always been so much clearer than mine.

"I don't want to go through this again," I say.

"I'm not asking you to be a parent."

"But I'm not just a donor here."

"You don't have to be involved."

"Emily, what kind of choice does that leave me?"

"I can do this on my own."

"And you think I could just walk away, abandon my own child?"

Max hollers into the silence that falls between us. "Mama! The water's cold!"

"Give me a minute," she says, wiping her thumbs under her eyes and reaching for a paper towel.

She turns around in the doorway just as she's leaving the kitchen. "You left because you wanted your freedom. You could at least give me the respect of letting me have mine. It doesn't have to be this complicated."

She clods up the stairs, not waiting for a response.

I grab my keys and leave the envelope exactly where it lies on the counter.

"Come on, sweetheart," I can hear her saying upstairs. "Here's the soap. Do your bits."

"This is the ocean," he says, "and I'm a shark. Soap is poison."

I walk out the front door before she's left the bathroom.

I'm pacing around the living room after dinner on Thursday, tidying up Max's toys, tossing Lego pieces and the limbs of various action figures into bins stored inside the ottoman. I pull a couple of books from the Lego bin and take them into the tiny second bedroom which is both my office and where

Max sleeps. The closet is full of toys Max has outgrown, and the bookshelf still holds some of his favourites from when he was younger: *Ferdinand* and *Clifford* alongside the few poorly produced books that make some attempt to depict alternative families, none of which quite looks like ours.

"Mom," says Max, coming into the room. "What about soccer?"

"Oh shit, sorry Max, what time is it?" We're late for his game.

"You sweared."

"Swore. And I'm sorry, honey. Just please don't repeat it."

Which is always a mistake. Half an hour later, as I'm desperately trying to find a place to park, out it comes from his mouth.

"Ugh. Maxi, please." I mime zipping my mouth shut.

"But you said it."

"I'm an adult."

"That's not fair."

"Yup. Come on, sweetheart, let's get you onto the field."

I return to the car and watch him, a speck of gold and blue, through the windshield. I should get out there and take my place among the dads. I'm not great at small talk at the best of times, but they're all decent guys. We wear the same shoes and usually stand around showing each other new apps on our iPhones and talking tech or sports.

Later, as I'm wrangling Max into his T-Rex PJs, he says, "Mom, do you hate Mama?"

"No, Max. What makes you say that?"

"You don't sound like *you* when you talk to her."

"How do I sound?"

"There's no song in your voice."

"That's my professor voice," I say, feeling awful and trying to explain it away.

"Are your students scared of you?"

I kiss the silken top of his head and say "Maybe sometimes, but you don't ever need to be."

—

I smell tuna fish as soon as I reach the door of Solomon's office. "Had lunch?" he asks, holding out half a sandwich on a piece of wax paper. A small carton of milk is open on his desk. Optics, I want to say to him. It's a little hard to take you seriously when it looks like your mother packed your lunch.

"I'm good, thanks," I say, digging a file out of my knapsack. I managed to get the paperwork by email from the clinic; the originals are somewhere in the house.

"My wife always used to say I used too much mayo."

"Past tense," I say, sliding the file across his desk.

"She died. Well, first she left me, then she died."

It doesn't surprise me that a man in this business has had his own share of family casualties.

He licks a fat thumb and quickly turns the pages, extracting one stapled set. He holds his glasses at a distance in order to magnify the print. "So you agreed to donate the embryos to research in the case of separation, divorce or death," he says.

"Yes."

"Okay," he says, leaning back, forefingers to his chin. "So say our argument is that you should both be bound by the contract you signed—what, seven, eight years ago? Before you had a child and several years before you separated."

"Right," I nod.

"Now, what if her lawyer comes back and says, 'Actually, my client wasn't truly in a position to give informed consent at the time, not without legal or psychological counsel. Perhaps she signed under duress, or in a state of some kind of psychological distress, anxious that if she didn't concur with your wishes you would withdraw what was then her closest chance to becoming a mother.' You see, as the non-biological partner, it could be argued that she was the one in the more vulnerable position. You had the certainty of the ability to conceive and of your genetic contribution to the embryos—what kind of certainty did she have?"

"Are you siding with her?"

"I'm speaking hypothetically. My own feeling is that the legal enforceability of these contracts is highly debatable for any number of reasons, some of which I am presenting here. But you do have to consider that your ex-partner will be seen to have rights of her own in this. Reproductive rights."

"That I will be seen to be denying her?"

"Here's the thing," says Solomon. "However impassioned and genuine your plea to have your ownership privileged over hers, the opposition will find ways to suggest an ulterior motive."

"But I don't have an ulterior motive."

"And yet you would rather see those embryos be given to science than go to your ex-partner."

I can feel myself flush with heat.

"Look, I'm being provocative, it's my job," he says, placing his palms on his desk. "Who among us has not experienced jealousy, a desire to seek retribution, an impulse to deny something to someone with whom we were once in an intimate relationship, to punish or hurt them in some way?"

"But I'm not trying to punish anyone," I say.

"What is it, then? What's this really about?"

"Well, we could start with the basic fact that the eggs were mine," I say.

Solomon sighs. "It's a flimsy argument."

"It doesn't feel flimsy."

"I appreciate that, but in a legal sense? —Look," he says, leaning in. "You can't argue for equal rights in theory and then say they don't work for you in reality."

I'm silent. So is he. I can hear the glugging of a water dispenser somewhere down the hall.

"I just don't have it in me to go through this again," I say quietly. "Not with Emily, not with anyone. None of it came naturally to me. It wasn't until Max was about four that I even understood how to be his parent. It tore Emily and me apart. And what about my career? Max is finally of an age where I have a bit more freedom."

"Okay," he says, "now you're building a more complex argument. While your ex-partner might have reproductive rights, you also have rights not to be compelled to be a parent."

"What does that mean, exactly?"

"It could mean a couple of things. Number one, she could free you of all parental obligations related to a second child, financial and otherwise."

"But you can't unburden yourself of the responsibility you feel in your bones, in your heart."

"Which brings me to number two, which is what I think you're getting at. You have the right not to be forced to assume the psychosocial burdens that come with being a genetic parent."

I let that sink in for a moment, then ask, "So, are you telling me I have a case?"

"Maybe take a couple of days to see how this argument sits with you. Do you know who's representing her?"

"Emily?" I shake my head. She won't have gone to a lawyer. She couldn't afford one and besides, she's much more likely to suggest counselling. Hiring a lawyer is just not her style.

ADAM

WHEN THE aggressively cheerful gay barista at the Starbucks around the corner from their new apartment asks him how he's doing, as he asks every morning, Adam is not supposed to pause and reflect, he is simply supposed to do his best impression of an American and say: "Great!"

This is what he reports to his psychiatrist, Renata, a woman he is obliged to see three times a week. See? it's as if he is saying. Look how much I'm learning about your alien ways, how quickly I am adapting. It's been most of a decade since I've been in the US for any length of time and it's not that things have changed so much, it's that I really don't belong here.

Adam remembers feeling similarly when he returned from Honduras as a graduate student—a detachment from his surroundings that made him question everything; a distinct disillusionment, cynicism, even, about the superficiality and wastefulness of American lives. At the time, he hadn't wanted to lose that perspective; perhaps that was part of the reason he had set his sights on the foreign service—he could see how quickly and easily one might become seduced by the relative comfort and ease of this place, how quickly one might become inured to the ills of the world.

Renata doesn't seem particularly interested in his vague philosophical commentary. She's always pressing for specifics, driving him like a train, getting him to describe every station in mundane detail, even those stations where the train never stopped—pointless details that get them nowhere, in Adam's opinion.

"You were telling me last time about the tension you could feel building in the camp," she says this morning. "I wonder if you might be able to describe the days leading up to your kidnapping."

The idea of going over this again exhausts him. "It's all in the debriefing," he says, pointing at a fat file on her desk. He'd gone over the chronology with both military and consular officials and a psychiatrist in Washington and he is pretty sure he isn't going to remember anything more or differently with another account.

He doesn't want to be here, but Renata is part of the deal he has made. The State Department will pay for language training, physio and his prosthesis, but he won't be considered for another overseas posting until he's gone through this and received a clean bill of psychological health. He doesn't even know how dirty the current bill is—for some ludicrous reason he is not allowed to know the details of the assessment that was undertaken by the psychiatrist in Washington six weeks ago.

"The facts are one thing," Renata says, "but it's very common to come away from a situation like this and still have difficulty making sense of it."

"It's not a complicated story," Adam insists. "I wasn't careful. I was kidnapped, and after some time, I was set free."

"But how did you feel about being taken hostage, Adam, about being captive? Angry? Ashamed? Afraid?"

"Afraid? My job always has an element of fear about it."

"You weren't just doing your job. You were taken out of your job, taken out of your life, in fact. It was a total disruption that plunged you into circumstances of considerable uncertainty, life-threatening uncertainty. In my experience, that kind of situation is generally traumatizing."

Even her mild expressions of sympathy irritate him. "You're making all sorts of assumptions here. What if I thrive in situations of considerable, even life-threatening uncertainty? What if this is exactly why I can do the work I do, why I'm any good at it at all?"

"Then I would think there was a history of trauma predating this most recent experience."

Adam rolls his eyes. "Look, I'm not doing this with you. I'm not going to delve into my childhood and tell you I had a mother who didn't love me or any of that kind of bullshit."

"What would you like me to know about your mother?" Renata says.

"Jesus Christ!" Adam shouts and stands up.

"Look," he says. "A kid, an innocent kid was killed because of me, killed making some kind of fucking vigilante move to save my life. A kid who was recruited by this terrorist organization because he had nothing, nothing else, who was exploited by everyone involved—have I told you? Have I even told you about Oskar?"

"Tell me about Oskar," she says.

Adam canes his way across the street to the bus stop after his appointment with Renata. It's one of those flat California days when the air is completely still and the sky is no colour at all. If Adam didn't have this structure imposed on his day, he'd find it difficult not to be plotting his escape.

For six hours a day he is studying at the DLI's Foreign Language Center alongside a bunch of military personnel a good deal younger. Seven men and five women, the brightest and the best, headed for jobs in military intelligence. They practice conversational Levantine Arabic in the mornings, then work on reading and writing classical Arabic in the afternoons.

Their teacher, Usted Bashir, a professor from the American University in Beirut, is a bit of a hard-ass, but he's got a kind of patrician charm. He pays Adam a little more respect than the others both because of his age and, he suspects, out of sympathy. Drew, the twenty-one-year-old midwesterner who sits beside Adam, is the only one who has dared ask about his leg. "IED?" he'd whispered on their first day, gesturing toward Adam's interim prosthesis.

Adam had nodded in reply.

He has the feeling his leg is supposed to bother him more than it does. He'd like to do without the cane, but he's quite confident that will come with physio. The stump has healed nicely after an initial infection, and he's almost ready to be fitted with a new prosthesis. He's specified that he doesn't want the cosmetic version, but the robotic-looking one: he doesn't feel a need to pretend to be like everyone else, or make other people comfortable.

He takes the prosthesis off when he gets home in the late afternoon, his stump sore, his brain a bit fried from all the conjugating of verbs. This is the hardest part of the day for him, when the Arabic leaves and Sofie is there and the sun is going down, heralding the long night ahead.

She is here in Monterey for him, with him, though it's not ideal for her: she has three regular shifts at the community hospital and she's on call five nights a week. She says she doesn't mind in the short term, but Adam finds it very hard not to let her sacrifices make him feel guilty, and then resentful.

"This is my choice," she says, whenever she can see Adam heading there, overwhelmed.

He is overwhelmed most of the time, it seems.

He doesn't want to talk when he gets home, he just wants quiet. But there is nothing quiet in his head once the night descends. It is like being down the well again, the world above on fire, with Oskar in the scene now, laughing at him from above. It is the sound of him Adam recognizes; Oskar's face is obscured by light and dark. He has a fantasy of reaching through the tunnel and the flames to place his hands around Oskar's throat and strangle the life out of him.

The man was evil. He said as much in his deposition to the State Department. But they were more interested in the Mullah. He was the one they were pursuing. They'd asked Adam to recall every detail of the Mullah's appearance in order to come up with a composite. It was accurate but generic. Like a cartoon cliché of a terrorist that might run in a French newspaper.

When they tried to create a composite of Oskar, though, they got it entirely wrong. Or Adam got it wrong. The details just didn't add up to create a portrait that resembled him, no matter what angle Adam considered.

—

Adam has admitted to a certain amount of terror at night and Renata has prescribed a combination antidepressant and anti-anxiety med with strict interdictions against alcohol. Adam isn't opposed to taking the pills, but while he's never been a heavy drinker, he has come to rely on half a bottle of vodka to take the edge off during the small-numbered hours when Sofie is asleep or at work.

Earlier in the evenings, after he and Sofie have eaten dinner, they watch something mindless, entangled together on the couch, often sliding into sex. For whatever reason, arousal hasn't failed him. He feels like this is the only place he and Sofie connect, where they fail to in other ways, especially those moments with too many words.

He can sleep for a while afterwards, but then he typically wakes sometime after midnight with a thundering heart and a gaping, hollow fear. He reorients himself—I am in the US, Sofie is asleep in the bedroom, I am safer than I have been in over a decade—and yet at night he can feel as if he is alone in the most hostile of places, alone and about to die. He pours vodka into his mouth and paces in front of the sliding glass doors to the balcony, needing the lights of the world but not finding much comfort in them, needing something he cannot name.

Oskar often appears as a dark presence at the edge of Adam's peripheral vision. In order to take control of Oskar's presence in his mind, Adam will turn to his laptop. He's determined to find him, expose his real identity; determined to hold him to account.

What he doesn't have at his disposal is the security clearance that once allowed him access to diplomatic channels. He would have started with the Norwegian embassies in Addis and Nairobi in that case. Instead, he began by working his way through the rosters of Norwegian NGOs and engineering companies working in East Africa. For such a small country, Norway certainly produces a lot of expats—but, as Adam suspected, he's found no evidence to suggest Oskar is one of them. So now he is on to *all* the NGOs and engineering companies working in East Africa, a considerably bigger undertaking.

He started with the foreign-owned or foreign-run outfits based out of Nairobi, the headquarters of most operations in the region. He's familiar with quite a few people in that world, but he just can't deal with having to summarize the last few months to another person. Can't deal with summary or sympathy. He selectively emails Wendell, an Australian mining guy, the toughest, least sentimental person he knows.

"Good to hear from you, mate," Wendell writes back. "I'll put out a couple of feelers."

Adam must have nodded off at some point in the night. Sofie enters the living room in a blue silk robe, her hair a morning mess of waves. She shuffles over and sits down in his lap.

"You didn't sleep at all, did you?" she says, running her hands through his hair.

Adam shrugs, growing hard.

"I'll make coffee," she says.

He pulls her back by the hand.

"I stopped taking the pill," she says.

"Do you want to get a condom?"

"No, I want you to come inside me. I want you as close as you can be."

—

In Renata's cream-coloured office, Adam tries to build a more three-dimensional portrait of Oskar. "I keep going over and over what I know about him, trying to figure him out, what all these pieces, these contradictions, add up to."

"I wonder, given your preoccupation with Oskar, whether he might represent some part of you," Renata says, leaning forward in her leather armchair.

"What do you mean, *part* of me?"

"Sometimes we split ourselves into different parts in order to survive."

"You think I made him up?"

"I'm not saying he wasn't real to you."

Adam starts to grow hot. "Look," he says. "Are you here to help me or challenge the veracity of what I'm telling you?"

"Do you feel I'm challenging it?"

Adam leans forward in his chair and stares deeply into the curious navy of her eyes, trying to find some truth, but there's an opaqueness there, no way in. Be careful, he thinks to himself. His future employment, deployment, is in her hands.

All he has is his memories of Oskar, nothing tangible he can point to and say, Here, this is the motherfucker I'm talking about.

"Listen, I know intelligence hasn't been able to ID him," Adam says, "but that doesn't mean anything. He could have any number of aliases."

"Like you did?"

Adam inhales, but can't seem to get enough air. He stands up and breathes as deeply as he can, the edges of his field of vision turning mustard-coloured, grainy.

"I work undercover," he says. "It's my job."

"It must get confusing managing different identities."

"It doesn't. No."

"Tell me about them," she says, "Adam and Daniel. How are they different? How are they the same?"

Adam slumps back down into the chair.

She is twisting things, he thinks, making inferences, getting him to fit into some diagnosis she already has in mind.

I'll fucking find Oskar, Adam thinks. I'll prove that he is real.

Oskar had mentioned two teenaged daughters in Bergen. And there was the twenty-six-year-old French girlfriend in Nairobi and the driver in Mogadishu who was one of forty-three children. There must be some elements of truth in this. Even under his aliases, Adam himself had kept certain core details consistent, principally the truth of both his parents being dead. It is better to have a couple of anchors in real life or the whole construct can be too flimsy.

He thunks down the street away from Renata's office in search of a big hit of caffeine. He eventually finds a coffee shop that isn't overwhelmed with twenty-somethings on their laptops, orders an Americano and sits down on a low couch. He picks up the front section of the *LA Times* but he can't focus.

He should be using this time to try and finish his Arabic homework, but this language learning is not going particularly well. When he's in class he can feel he just has a grasp of the grammar, but he loses hold of it the minute he steps out of the room. The script can be confounding, with too many letters looking too similar and the absence of written vowels. He stares at his homework at the end of the day and thinks:

I might as well be looking at a school of fish. After a bit of time, if he's lucky, he'll notice one of those fish has a tail unlike the others. It's such slow and painful work.

He's not going to get to his homework or his classes today. He's got too much to do. Before looking into Oskar's personal relationships, he should compile a list of all foreigners who have been kidnapped by al-Shabaab—the ones who survived, anyway. If Oskar was actually working for or with al-Shabaab, some other captive might have suffered his acquaintance.

At the public library on Pacific Street, Adam sits crammed between a heavily perfumed middle-aged woman updating her CV and a homeless man watching a video about sea urchins. He slouches and lowers his head, as self-conscious doing this research in public as he would be watching porn. It is a mistake, in any case. Almost every search related to kidnapping and Somalia turns up stories about Daniel Rainier, the missing American aid worker now presumed dead.

He gets up and goes outside to clear his head, standing under the overhang out of the drizzle. An old bearded guy in a wheelchair asks him if he has a smoke. Adam shakes his head.

"How much that cost you then?" he says, pointing at Adam's prosthesis.

"It was covered," Adam says, feeling immediately guilty. He can imagine how it must look to a guy like this. He's wearing jeans, but his legs lie flat.

"Vietnam," the guy says. "You?"

Adam can't compare war stories. This guy has a war story. Adam's is the story of an overeducated white guy who got a huge tax-free salary and became a little too confident and cocky and now has a psychiatrist, physiotherapist and prosthetist piecing him back together courtesy of a government that paid two million dollars for his release.

"Car accident," Adam says, giving him twenty bucks.

He doesn't mean to be patronizing. He knows there is nothing he can give the guy that would make up for the disparity between them. Nobody's life is worth as much as his has cost.

—

They have rented a car for the day to take the scenic route to Carmel. It was Sofie's idea—she thinks it will do them good to spend the day together by the ocean. Adam has to refrain from telling Sofie how to drive. He will be able to drive with his prosthetic leg eventually, his physiotherapist assures him, but his phantom foot twitches for the pedal right now.

In Kenya, Adam had had a driver who showed him how to navigate the roads, dodge the stray dogs and cattle, overtaking diesel-spewing buses with people clinging to their exteriors, men hanging from the window ledges by their fingernails, feet grazing the ground around corners. Whenever he was needed on the coast, though, he preferred to take the overnight train from Nairobi to Mombasa, its slow churning the perfect accompaniment to his otherwise least-favourite activity: the writing of reports.

He has never slept better than he did on that train, gently rocking in a top bunk, the window of the compartment open, the vegetation growing so thick and close to the tracks in some parts that he could reach his hand over his head and run his fingers through it. He ate chapattis with chai for breakfast, bought from a couple of kids running beside the tracks through a dusty town, passing a handful of shillings through the window.

Sofie is quiet until they are on the highway. Then she reaches over to take Adam's hand.

"I want us to try and have a baby, Adam. I'm thirty-nine. If we don't try now, it'll probably never happen."

"I thought you felt there were already too many children in the world."

"I want your child. All those months when I thought I could lose you, I kept thinking about it. It was like this fantasy that kept me going."

"I didn't realize."

"Adam, I understand the PTSD. I know you are going through a lot. But I think it would be good for us to have a new, totally different, shared adventure. A little person in the world made up of both of us."

"But what about your work?"

"My work is here now," she says. "Our lives are here now. It makes other things possible."

Adam is looking at the road, the greyness of it, wondering: But where? Where is here? What is here? It can't end here. He doesn't think it can even begin here. This is just a place in between.

Adam nods his head, less as an expression of agreement than as an overture to silence.

LILA

ROBIN IS on her way to Istanbul. Her father had apparently abducted her from her mother when she was just two years old. He brought her from Turkey to Canada where he'd kept her hidden in a basement apartment for nine years, away from people and sunlight. She had never learned English, but her father used to leave a radio on behind a locked door when he went out to work. So she had not just a spider, but muffled music and commentary for company.

One night, her father hadn't come home and for the first time, she'd found the door to the stairwell unlocked.

After escaping, she'd been afraid to speak at all; afraid to be sent back to her father.

The police have not been able to locate him, but they were able to find her mother in Turkey through Interpol. She had reported her daughter's disappearance years ago. She had never given up hope.

There was no possibility of my saying goodbye. Mirabelle had shuttled a screaming Robin out of the office. Jacqui had stopped my forward momentum by saying my name so sternly and at such volume that a plainclothes officer had stood up and asked if she needed assistance. She'd pointed him toward a struggling Mirabelle, and he'd moved in and escorted them out of the building.

I've been lying in a puddle on my couch for an entire month. I lie here and imagine I have nothing more than a spider for company. I turn on my father's radio in the next room and listen to it through the wall.

Jacqui comes by to see me because I'm not answering my phone. She brings a tourtière and a salad and opens a window and washes all the cups on the counter. I haven't been drinking: I don't even have the energy to get to the liquor store.

Jacqui doesn't seem angry with me, though she must be putting aside massive disappointment; she says she is seriously concerned. In the short term she wants me to get on some antidepressants. In the longer term she wants me to work with a therapist and address what happened with Robin—the countertransference, the re-enactment of something informed, she is quite sure, by some early failure of attachment.

Her language feels far too abstract and theoretical, addressed to a part of my brain that is, for the time being, absent. I can feel my eyes fluttering with exhaustion as she speaks. She apologizes, and tries to simplify it for me. "You need to talk to someone about your own experience of being abandoned and adopted." She sits down beside me as I close my eyes. She takes my hand and holds it for a very long time.

Just before she is about to leave she says we might need to talk about my disciplinary review hearing next month. My ability to practice has been suspended with an allegation of professional misconduct. "I can have it postponed until you're feeling a bit more resilient," she offers.

I just nod. Do I even care? Am I really going to go through the humiliation of a review hearing again? Do I have it in me to argue my case? I had admitted to boundary violations where Izzie and her father were concerned, but I hadn't had an affair with Izzie's father. It had come down to Lori's word against mine. But in Robin's case, I have no defence.

I might need a job that is just a job, one where I'm not a danger to myself and others. For the time being, I've got some of my mother's investments to keep me afloat.

What is the point of a human life unrelated to any other human life? I keep thinking. What is the point of mine? It can feel like I'm little more than a speck of flotsam floating over an ocean in which I can't swim. I am missing something that other humans possess, some essential weight or centre that would root me in time and space.

"I'm writing you a prescription," Jacqui says, pulling a pad out of her purse. "And I'm going to refer you to a colleague at the hospital."

After a few weeks on the pills, the sky does seem clearer. It's only then that I can admit the truth to myself. I'd wanted to be a mother to a child who had experienced her deepest injuries elsewhere, rather than be the one responsible for the psychic damage I would undoubtedly cause a child of my own.

I still want to be a mother, but I'm afraid. As this plays out in my mind over the next couple of weeks, the skies seem to grow even clearer, revealing a shade of blue I am certain I have never seen before. I make a doctor's appointment then—not with the psychiatrist Jacqui has referred me to, but with a fertility specialist instead.

—

The fertility clinic is on the upper floors of a sterile office building downtown. I wonder if the people working in the offices below have any idea what goes on upstairs.

The doctor has me undergo a month of cycle monitoring first in order to ensure everything is working as it should. I join a silent stream of women pouring into the elevator between six and seven a.m. every morning. On the eleventh floor, I stand in line with a dozen other women waiting for blood tests. After three vials are drawn, I take a seat in a hard plastic white chair to await my turn for an ultrasound, the generic murmur of televised cooking shows in the background.

Everyone waits in silence, flicking idly through texts, each woman with her own complicated story avoiding making eye contact with other women and their equally complicated stories. I can feel the heartbreak and the hope in the room.

On day fifteen of my cycle, one good-sized egg drops. I'm still uncertain about which donor to choose. I'm looking through a catalogue of thousands, wondering: Do you look for the same qualities you might look for in a partner? Should you choose a donor you might be willing to have sex with in real life? That just feels wrong: the men are twenty years younger than me. What about his grades, higher education, aptitude for sports or music? None of these are strictly genetically determined; most of them depend at least as much upon the environment in which you grow up.

I've run out of time for deliberations. I need to choose a donor before an egg drops next month. I decide that in addition to reasonable looks, and a good medical and genetic history, I want a donor who seems to know himself. A slightly older donor—and by older I mean in his mid-twenties rather than his late-teens—might have had more time to consider the implications.

The donor I finally choose seems intelligent and clear-eyed. In his essay he is up front in saying that while this is a way for him to pay for graduate school, he genuinely hopes that families who need help in this regard can benefit from something that would otherwise go to waste. I like his pragmatism, the lack of romance or ego. I like that one of us, at least, seems unafraid.

I purchase six units of his sperm from a warehouse in Atlanta that stores donations made at various clinics throughout the US and Canada—six, because it is cheaper to buy in bulk, and who knows how many tries it will take? As the fertility doctor has repeatedly told me, at forty my chances of conceiving in any given month are only about five to seven percent. I opt for the more expensive option of having the samples washed free of seminal fluid and slow swimmers, samples that can be inserted directly into the cervix. Why bother, after all, with the gunk? I like the idea that the money my mother left me is paying for this, even though she set aside a great deal more money for an organization that plants trees in Israel.

And so the waiting in line early every morning for blood tests and ultrasounds begins again the following month. A technician measures the burgeoning follicles, the blood tests indicate my FSH levels are good and the doctor predicts insemination will likely take place around day fourteen of my cycle.

I've been focused on the clinical aspects of this experience, the science, but this is suddenly about to become very real. I lie awake doubting myself, feeling anxious. How can I possibly be a mother? I'm not even good at taking care of myself. And on my own? Without the mitigating presence of a partner? What am I thinking? Maybe the longing I felt to adopt Robin doesn't translate into a desire for my own child. Maybe it doesn't mean the same thing at all.

The morning of what is to be the sixth ultrasound this month, I'm in the waiting room, fumbling for my phone in my purse, when I spill a bit of my coffee onto the lap of the woman waiting next to me. I apologize over and over, digging into my jacket pocket for a Starbucks napkin I know I have stuffed in there, but she just brushes the coffee off with the back of her hand and says: "These jeans are so old I should have chucked them out ages ago." Not the slightest bit of annoyance. She just folds her hands back in her lap and gazes at the framed poster of ducks on a mist-covered pond on the far wall, a small, contented smile on her face.

I stare at her: this portrait of quiet, radiant calm. I have this overwhelming sense that she is meant to be here while I am not. This isn't just about science to her; this is about love. Everything about me seems to be about love's absence.

I don't want to up the dose of my antidepressants while I'm trying to conceive, but I find myself feeling increasingly despondent and lonely on these mornings amongst women who seem to have no doubts about why they're here.

A couple of days later, I get the call that a good egg is about to drop. I go into the clinic at noon the next day to be inseminated. The doctor gives me a tiny plastic vial to warm up in my hand—one unit of frozen sperm that has been sent from Atlanta by FedEx—and here I am thawing it between my palms.

The whole experience has all the romance of getting a pap smear, right down to the cold metal of the forceps, a remote twinge of pain and the bright fluorescent light. I linger a minute in the room afterwards wondering why it leaves me feeling so empty.

I occupy myself for the next couple of weeks with some administration, writing a letter to the provincial regulatory board to let them know I won't be proceeding with the hearing and I won't be looking to have my status reinstated. I do my taxes. I try to make a list of transferable skills but come up very short. I try to think of what else I might possibly be qualified to do. I wonder, in addition to typing like a demon, what one needs to become a court stenographer.

Then I pee on a stick and, because I can't believe the result, I go to the clinic to have a blood test. In the face of all the foreboding statistics for women my age, I am actually pregnant. The doctor sees me to discuss next steps, but I am still stuck on this one. She tells me that at my next appointment, in six weeks' time, she'll be able to measure the embryo's heartbeat. This is all happening so fast, too fast.

"Is this the news you were expecting?" she asks, unable to gauge my reaction.

"I'm surprised," is all I manage.

"Sometimes it's hard to commit to the reality of it until the first trimester is over," she says, sliding a new page of alarming statistics across the table.

"Is there anyone you want to call with the news?"

I shake my head and thank her, folding the piece of paper and putting it into my purse.

As the doors of the elevator slide closed I break down in tears, shrinking down against the glass wall. When the elevator slows at the fourth floor, I quickly reach out and press the emergency button. I just want things to stand still for a moment before the doors open to the world. The elevator hisses to a rumbling stop.

It comes over me again—I am terrified of having my own child. I hadn't been terrified of the idea of adopting Robin; the damage had been done elsewhere; I would have been the one to heal rather than harm her. But I hadn't been that, had I. I had used her for my own purposes, misled her, lied to everyone involved.

I am vaguely aware of the sound of an alarm. A voice through a speaker above me. And suddenly I'm acutely embarrassed by my rashness, by my lack of explanation for the security guard who pries open the elevator doors, by his accusation of public mischief, by the sight of a paramedic and the fact that I cannot stop crying.

"You coming from the eleventh floor?" the paramedic asks me gently.

I nod meekly.

"Is there someone I can call for you?"

Solomon is who I call. He has me get in a cab and come to his office. And then he picks up the phone and calls Dr. Heinz, the colleague Jacqui referred me to four months ago.

ADAM

IN RENATA'S waiting room, Adam is staring at a framed poster of two bodies entwined in some complicated dance. It's the first time he has noticed it. Adam wonders whether all psychiatrists hang such bad art. This crap and the old *New Yorkers* with the address labels blacked out and the Kleenex box with its tatty homemade crocheted cover and the beige chairs, and beige walls, and beige carpet—the generic liberalism and nothingness of colour are pissing him off this morning.

As is the fact that someone very agitated is stomping around in Renata's office at this moment. Even worse—she is wailing. Although it feels kind of creepy to listen, Adam can't help leaning forward in his chair. She's sobbing, great dramatic crescendos of heaving pain, and Adam thinks: Jesus Christ, is that how I'm meant to behave in there?

The woman throws the door open so hard it slams into the wall. Adam holds his breath, watching her feet as she crosses the beige and exits the waiting room.

"I'll be right with you, Adam," says Renata's disembodied voice, calm and business-as-usual.

She is standing in the doorway a minute later in all her Boho glory: Birkenstocks, neutral linens and chunky "ethnic" jewellery. Adam can imagine her as one of those strange tall, genderless women from Denmark and Germany who fall in love with Masai warriors and take up residence in the family kraal.

"Does that woman always have the appointment before me?"

"Sorry to have kept you waiting," she says.

Adam makes a point of looking around the office today. Better art in here. He stretches out his prosthetic leg in order to ease a prickling sensation that tends to happen if he sits in one position for any length of time.

"Is your leg bothering you?" Renata asks.

"Pins and needles."

"I've noticed you don't talk much about your leg."

Adam shrugs. "I'm at physio twice a week. That's plenty of talking about my leg."

"About the physical, I'm sure," says Renata. "But what about the emotional?"

"Would you believe me if I said I was okay with it?"

She purses her lips. "I would think that was a defence," she says.

But Adam's new prosthesis has his admiration and respect;

it is one very sophisticated piece of machinery and it has been so meticulously crafted that it fits beautifully, too.

"Part of our work together involves helping you adjust to this new reality," Renata says.

"My new life as a superhero?" he says. "Seriously, have you ever seen that South African guy—the blade runner? He's making a bid for the Olympics—not the Paralympics, but the *Olympics*."

"Did you want to be a superhero when you were a boy?"

"Doesn't everyone?"

"Who did you want to be?"

"Superman."

"Someone with two identities."

Oh fuck, Adam thinks.

Renata looks at him in that opaque psychiatric way she has, waiting for him to say something more. Adam stares right back, thinking: You are not going to pin me with some personality disorder in addition to PTSD.

He's got to find another way to get to Oskar. It will be pretty near impossible to find his alleged family. What about the driver in Mogadishu? Adam could get in touch with every aid agency and foreign company in the battered capital and say he is looking for a recommendation for a driver, someone who has worked with foreigners before.

He looks at the clock: thirty minutes to go. This is such a waste of time.

"Where did you go, Adam?" Renata asks.

He just shakes his head. A man has a right to his privacy.

When he gets home that night he goes straight for the vodka, not even bothering with ice.

"Babe," says Sofie, sitting down on the arm of his chair, her hand wrapped around a mug of tea. "I went back to the doctor today."

Adam looks at her blankly. Has she been to the doctor recently?

"Remember I told you I thought I should have some tests done on account of my age?"

Wait a minute, he thinks, how long ago did Sofie stop taking the pill? "It hasn't been very long, has it?"

"It's been a while," she says. "Anyway, I got the results."

"Yeah?" he says, inhaling.

"A couple of polyps, but really small and nowhere near the ovaries, so it's unlikely they're getting in the way. So—" she says with some hesitation, "—the doctor suggested we do a sperm analysis to just like, you know, rule anything out."

"But there's nothing wrong with my sperm."

"How can you be so sure?"

"I was a sperm donor when I was a grad student."

Sofie stands up and steps back. "Why have you never told me that?"

"It didn't seem relevant. It was just something I did for money a long time ago."

She immediately reddens and clenches her hands together.

"Sofie, come on. It just hasn't come up before. I don't even think about it. In any case, my point is, they don't just take anybody as a donor. I had like, superior-quality sperm."

She covers her mouth with her hand and for a moment Adam can't tell if she's going to laugh or cry. She turns away, interlacing her fingers as she grips the back of her head.

He says her name a couple of times, unsure of what to do. "Sofie, where is this all coming from? Why this sudden desire to have a child?"

Sofie catches her breath. "Things change, Adam," she says. "I lived for months with the terror of losing you—do you have any idea what that was like for me?"

"I'm sorry."

"It doesn't require an apology. But can you understand how the experience led me to want something more permanent? A home, a family. Don't you want that too, Adam? After everything you've been through?"

How is it that I felt closer to Sofie when I was captive in Somalia, thousands of miles and so much uncertainty between us? he wonders. How is the idea of something stronger and more sustaining than the reality of it? It strikes him that they have lived more in the realm of ideas than reality for most of the time they have known each other. Now it is Sofie's idea of having a baby. Even sex will now be burdened with the weight of an idea.

She turns to the window. In the reflection he sees she is crying. He knows he is supposed to go and comfort her, reassure her, tell her yes, we will do this, find a way. But has she forgotten how most of the world's children live? Does she think she can just hive herself off from the ugly reality of the world? He knows he can't. He is part of that ugly reality, stained by its blood.

Sofie grabs a dishtowel from the kitchen and wipes her face. "Help me figure out if there's a problem. If you can't do it for us, Adam, can you do it for me?" she finally says, her voice sober now, exhausted.

He nods. Okay. That much he can do.

—

Yesterday Adam did as Sofie had asked and jerked off into a sterile plastic container with an orange lid in a pornographic closet at the hospital. They didn't have this kind of library when he was a grad student. Now there's a menu at the touch of a button with something appealing to every kind of taste. He opted for the buffet—Sorority Orgy. In the decade and a half he has been living outside of the US, pubic hair seems to have disappeared. He was a little taken aback by the prevalence of vaginal piercings. He scrolled back to the menu and found something a little more old-fashioned: Delivery Man.

This morning Adam is idly flipping through the paper at the library with too many unformed thoughts in his head. After sending out an avalanche of emails, he now has a list of seventeen drivers in Mogadishu, ten of them named Mohammed. He has managed to reach five of them so far, posing as a Norwegian engineer named Hans.

"You might have driven for a colleague of mine a while ago, a white-haired Norwegian named Oskar," he tries with each one.

He's had five maybes, which he takes as nos, because no one wants to disappoint. Five maybes and five exorbitant quotes for daily rates in US dollars. War is good for business.

He's ditching therapy today. He's not interested in sharing any of this with Renata and he has zero interest in talking about what's going on with Sofie, either. She has thrown herself into "preparing the nest," as she calls it, modifying her diet, taking various supplements and isolating muscles well out of sight. He's finding it obsessive and stifling: she has asked for his support in cutting out alcohol and caffeine.

When Adam was coming into the building a couple of hours ago, he spotted the same old grizzled vet in the wheelchair parked outside. It's bothering him now, the awareness of the guy's presence out there, trying to bum a smoke, a hat with a few quarters in it sitting in his lap.

Adam finds the guy parked in exactly the same spot as he was when he passed him earlier.

"Hey," the guy says. "How's the Bionic Man?"

Adam shrugs. "How 'bout you?"

"Seen better days."

"You from Monterey?" Adam asks.

"Naah. Midwest. Weather's better here."

"How long were you in Vietnam?"

"Did two tours. Second one got cut short."

"You must have seen some stuff."

"Ah, you don't want to know, buddy. No one should see that shit. Fucks you up for life."

He bums a smoke from an acne-covered kid then asks: "What's your story? I see you here every day. Lose your job or something?"

"I lost—I don't know—the point or something."

"Hah! There is no point," he says, chuckling. "No point in even thinking about it. You just carry on."

Adam thinks about this, wondering if it's constitutional. His father couldn't find it in himself to just carry on, after all.

"Can I ask you something?" he says to the vet. "Do you ever think about not carrying on?"

"Nope," he says without qualification. "Just not in my DNA, man."

Adam has to fight against the worry that it just might be in his.

—

After eleven maybes, one of the drivers Adam contacted reaches out to him in the night. He says he knows the man Adam is talking about—a foreigner, a Muslim with two wives.

This makes sense to Adam, but he wants to make sure they are talking about the same man. "Could you describe him to me?" he asks.

"Very very tall," says the driver.

Is he? Adam wonders. Adam is 6′2″ himself. "What about his hair, his eyes?"

"I never see."

"Yet you know he is very tall."

"Everyone know him. They call him *shajaratu abyad*—the tree who is white."

Adam pauses: it's beginning to sound a bit mythological. What if all these men Adam has contacted have been talking among themselves? In fact, what if this guy has been tasked with luring him to Mogadishu with the myth of the white tree?

"Do you know where I could find him?"

"You send me fifty thousand US and I find him, inshallah."

Adam feels his eyelids fluttering. He takes the dummy phone and smashes it down hard on the coffee table. He has nothing, nothing to prove Oskar's existence, only the shadowy shape of him in his head.

He's missed a second appointment with Renata now. Three strikes and he'll be out. He's begun to wonder if, when he entered Renata's office for the first time, she was already of the opinion, fed by the psychiatrist he'd seen in Washington for an initial assessment, that Oskar was some kind of delusion. Why was he never allowed to know what was in the Washington report? He wonders if any of the military or consular officials he spoke to ever even believed him—if they had, wouldn't they have pursued some kind of investigation into Oskar in addition to the Mullah?

Adam puts his palms over his ears and shakes his head hard. Then he leans over and smacks his forehead repeatedly against the coffee table. His blood speckles the guts of the dummy phone.

TESS

MAX IS trouncing me at Super Mario Galaxy tonight. The Cosmic Guide keeps appearing to try and help me out, but my head is in some other galaxy. I totally underestimated Emily. A registered letter arrived earlier today from a lawyer she appears to have engaged.

"Ooh," said Solomon, when I called to tell him. "So she's bringing the big guns."

We made an appointment for tomorrow morning and I googled this woman immediately after hanging up the phone. She's some hard-core advocate who has launched more than one constitutional challenge on behalf of same-sex couples. And she's won every time. Emily isn't messing around. I never knew she had this in her.

As I'm putting Max to bed I remind him that we need to sort out his clothes for an indoor soccer tournament in

Niagara Falls this weekend. I get a less than enthusiastic grunt in reply.

"I thought you were looking forward to it. You get to stay in a hotel, and you'll see the Falls and everything."

While it's only one night, it will be the first time he's been away from us both. I ask him whether he needs snacks for the bus and what the sleeping arrangements will be and get little more than "dunno" for answers.

I kiss him goodnight. We'll talk about it some more tomorrow. I hope he can get to sleep.

Solomon's office is more chaotic than usual. His desk is covered in banker's boxes. He apologizes for the mess and suggests we take our meeting to the boardroom on the floor below. He'll send for some coffee.

"Are you retiring?" I ask, as we descend in the elevator. I try not to stare at the vulnerably bald back of his head reflected in the elevator's mirrored walls.

"Cutting back a bit to spend some time with my grandkids."

"That's admirable," I say.

"It's compensatory. I wasn't really around for my kids, worked all the time. I didn't realize how quickly it was all going to pass."

The decision seems to have relieved him of some years. He's looking less like an old man today, doing without suspenders and wearing a smart blue shirt with whimsical cufflinks in the shape of little penguins.

The receptionist brings coffee and oatmeal cookies into the boardroom. Solomon reaches for a cookie and swiftly dips it into his coffee. He's in a reflective mood this morning. "The decision to scale back didn't come easily," he confesses. "I don't know myself unless I'm working."

I understand. It's the only way I feel grounded. I've been doing the bare minimum, neglecting my research entirely. I had planned to make two trips to Sudbury this fall to begin field research at my second site—an island in the middle of a wide river that was home to a small religious sect in the 1970s. If I don't get to Sudbury this month, it will be inaccessible until late spring.

"How did you get to that decision, then?" I ask Solomon.

"Here's what I do with any tough decision," he says, waving his cookie in the air. "I ask myself: What's the worst that can happen? What's the best? And what's the most likely?" He takes a bite of his cookie and crumbs tumble down his shirt.

In my situation, the easiest of those questions for me to answer is the third one. "I think the most likely scenario, in our case, honestly, is that it doesn't work. The embryo doesn't implant. There is no baby."

"So maybe you just roll the dice," he says with a shrug. "Odds are in your favour."

"That doesn't sound very lawyerly."

"You know the expression 'the law is a blunt instrument'? I am guilty of having used a sledgehammer myself, but when my own daughter was having marital difficulty? I told her to go see a rabbi rather than a lawyer."

If he said that to everyone he'd be out of a job. I wonder if this has anything to do with Emily having enlisted the "big guns." "Why are you saying this?"

He casts his gaze out the window. "Trust me, I've seen the worst of humanity doing the work that I do. I would like to spare you ever knowing that capacity in yourself."

"Why should I be spared?"

"Because I like you, kid."

I laugh, a bit embarrassed. *Kid*. I don't think anyone's ever called me that. Not even when I was one.

Max's mood doesn't rally over the next couple of days. He boards the bus early on Saturday morning, leaving me with a limp wave. In his absence, I do my best to plow my way through some reading, but I'm distracted and unable to concentrate.

I'm not entirely surprised when my phone rings at eleven p.m. It's one of Max's coaches. Max has apparently broken out in hives and started vomiting. I tell the coach I'm on my way. I get in my car immediately, not even bothering to change out of my pyjamas, hurtling west down the QEW.

An hour and fifteen minutes later, I take the turnoff to Niagara Falls a little too quickly, not realizing it's covered in a slick of ice until it's too late. I hit the brakes and the car starts to turn, gliding in circles, looping, and while I'm conscious of what is happening, it's as if I'm observing it; I've lost all control of the car and I'm wondering whether Max brought his stuffed T. Rex to camp and chastising myself for not having changed over to snow tires yet when the car slides against the guardrail and screeches to a stop.

I put my hazard lights on and reach over to the passenger side to roll down the window and have a look, somehow not registering until a few minutes later that the passenger door is folded in. I try the key in the ignition, but while the battery works, the engine is dead. I see lights in the rear-view mirror then; a car has pulled over about ten feet behind me. I step out of the car, wave my arms, and a young guy runs up saying "holy shit, man" and it's only then that my heart starts to pound.

"You gotta call the police," the guy says. Seeing me standing there mutely, he reaches into his pocket for his phone.

But I've got to get to Max. And I've got to wait for the police. And I don't have a car I can drive. I don't know what to do.

"Come get in my car, it's freezing out here," says the guy. "They'll be here in a few."

Once inside his car he asks if there's anyone I want to call. "Yeah," I mumble. "Yeah."

Two hours later, I'm in the backseat of Emily's car (our car, it used to be), Max nuzzled into my coat, crying and embarrassed. He's saying he got really itchy and then he barfed two times and he wanted to come home and he's sorry and he doesn't want the other kids to think he's a baby.

"You have nothing to apologize for," I assure him as we drive back down the black highway. "Everyone gets sick. They'll understand. You just want your own bed when you feel miserable."

I want my own bed. It's only now, with the familiarity of our car, a mix of coconut air freshener and Emily's perfume in the air, Emily driving, Max beside me, that I've started to feel shaky. What if I'd been seriously injured? What if I'd just bled to death in my car, Max waiting anxiously with his coach for a mother who never arrived?

When we get to the house, Max asks me to come in. Emily shrugs and opens the door.

She makes Max a cup of hot chocolate while he sits on a stool at the kitchen island and asks him whether something happened at camp, whether anyone was a bully, who he was sharing a room with, how they did in their afternoon game.

"I just got itchy and then I barfed," is all he offers. "It was gross, all orange, because we had mac and cheese for dinner."

"Thanks for the visuals," Emily says. "Listen, we should get you up to bed. It's super late."

"No," he says weakly.

"No?"

"Can we just watch a movie?"

"I should probably be going," I say.

"No," he says. "All of us."

And so the three of us sit down on the couch and watch *Despicable Me* until six a.m. Max falls asleep with his head in Emily's lap while she strokes his forehead, his feet buttressed against my thigh.

I peel myself away eventually and Emily stands up and stretches.

"Have you told him what's going on?" I ask at the front door.

"Are you saying you think that's what this is about?"

"I just wondered what he knows."

"He might sense something is up between us, but no, obviously I'm not going to say anything prematurely. I don't want to get his hopes up. I don't want to disappoint him. He's been on at me about a sibling for years."

"Has he?"

"He draws pictures of his ideal family. There's a dog named Popeye and a little brother he calls Jack. I even hear him talking to Jack sometimes."

This kind of crushes me. What else does he feel he has to keep from me?

"Look," says Emily, "I think Max understands you're a bit of a lone wolf, but life doesn't have to be as lonely as you insist on making it."

"I make it lonely?"

"Oh come on. The mothers' group? The parents of Max's friends? Even the *idea* of his potentially having half-siblings out there in the world had you reeling. You just dismiss people and possibilities out of hand."

"That's not entirely true."

"It's about something bigger than you, Tess—building a sense of community around your child, *for* your child. But you just continually shut down any potential for that. Get over yourself. Or don't. Fake it for Max—maybe it will rub off on you a bit. God forbid, maybe you'll even make a friend."

ADAM

SOMETHING INSTINCTIVE draws Adam down to the water. The sky is a rare uninterrupted blue, the ocean less agitated than usual. He takes a seat on a bench, the wharf to his left, a cluster of sea lions baking in the sun on a protected area of beach to his right. Great lumbering missiles of blubber. Our ancestors, he supposes; prehistoric mammals of the sea.

There's a white ship floating on the horizon, on its way, perhaps, to Asia. Adam's experience really doesn't go further east than Afghanistan and he's not really sure how that knowledge would translate to the rest of the world. China is all over East Africa now, in mining and infrastructure, creating a generation of fatherless half-Chinese Africans who are being neglected and shunned. We're such sloppy creatures, men, he thinks. What is the point of us? To just keep producing children? But we don't even take care of the ones we have.

Dr. Escobar had called up magnified microscopic images of Adam's sperm on his computer screen at their appointment this morning. Adam looked at all those black tadpoles swimming in grey and thought: How random we all are, how unlikely.

"There are certainly a lot of them," Sofie said, smiling at Dr. Escobar.

"Ah, yes," Dr. Escobar said, with just enough condolence in his voice that Sofie shifted forward to perch on the edge of her chair. "I'm afraid this is a classic picture of necrosis."

Adam reached to pick at the bandage that covered half his forehead. He'd told Sofie he'd stumbled in the night on the way to the bathroom without his prosthesis. His head was throbbing. As the doctor spoke, it was as if he was offering confirmation of something Adam already knew: something inside him was dead.

"But how? Why?" Sofie asked.

"Any number of reasons," said the doctor. "Age, genetics, environmental factors, radiation, infection, certain diseases, injury."

Five or six out of seven, thought Adam.

"It could be a short-term issue," said Dr. Escobar with a shrug. "I've seen plenty of men start producing healthy sperm after a necrotic period."

"How likely is that?" Sofie asked.

Adam had a hazy feeling of his absence from the room, none of his senses attuned to the environment.

"We can monitor things," Dr. Escobar said. "We can isolate healthy sperm as we find them. There are options."

"That's good," Sofie nodded. "Right, Adam?" she said, putting her hand on his thigh.

Adam forced a smile he knew was not going to convince anyone.

"After you've discussed how you want to proceed you can let me know," Dr. Escobar said then, removing himself from the conversation.

They left his office in silence, sharing the elevator ride down with another equally silent couple. Sofie leaned in and kissed him quickly on the lips when they reached the sidewalk. She had to get to work. "We'll talk about it tonight, okay?" she said. "Don't get discouraged. You heard what he said—options."

The thought of a conversation about this with Sofie exhausts him. What is he supposed to say to her? That the world might be better off if more sperm proved necrotic? Maybe this is an indication of the future: a harbinger of the species' end.

He leans back and eventually falls asleep on the bench, waking well into the afternoon. Someone has planted a large bottle of water by his head, assuming him homeless, perhaps. What he actually wants is a beer. He makes his way to a grocery store and buys four cans, stuffing them into his knapsack, and then walks up to the library.

The vet is sitting there in the late afternoon sun with his eyes closed. Adam pulls a cold can from his knapsack and puts it into his hand. His eyes flutter open and he squints into the sun, raising his other hand to shield his eyes.

"Fella," he says, looking at the can and quickly tucking it behind his back: "you'll get me turfed off my spot. Follow me around the bushes back there," he says with a jerk of his head. He tilts and wheels that chair like he's on a basketball court, lunging behind the bushes of a small parkette.

"Not that I'm not grateful," he says, raising the can, and pulling it open with a whoosh.

"Sorry, that was stupid of me."

"There's just a certain etiquette, you know?"

He nods. "I never introduced myself. Adam," he says, extending his hand.

The guy in the wheelchair reaches forward, his knuckles smudged with tattoos. "First man, huh?" he says. "I'm Pete, Pete Morelli." He tilts his head back and pours most of the contents of the can right down his throat.

"So how much d'ya get from the insurance?" he says.

"Listen, Pete. I wasn't entirely straight with you. I got an infection and had to have it amputated."

"I'm not judging anyone. We all got our crosses," Pete says, crushing the can in his tattooed paw. "Right. Thanks, man. I'm gonna head home now."

Adam's a little surprised, maybe a little disappointed by Pete's abrupt departure. "Do you want another?" he asks, reaching for his knapsack.

"Bring it with you," he says, wheeling off up Pacific Avenue. "It's not far," he yells over his shoulder. He beelines uphill, God his arms must be strong, and turns onto a path that runs beside a white clapboard house.

"I guess no one would pay for a motorized chair?" Adam says, following him down the path to the back of the house.

"Nah, but who wants it? You see the guys in the motorized ones? They're all flabby, outta shape. Not me."

He wheels up a makeshift ramp, flinging open an unlocked door, entering an enclosed back porch. It's a rectangular space with a sagging couch at one end, a hot plate and small fridge in the other, a brick wall and a bank of windows. Must get really cold in here, thinks Adam. He wonders if Pete has access to a bathroom.

"Make you something to eat?"

"That's okay," Adam says, shaking his head.

"You sure?" Pete says, pulling a container out of the fridge. "Make this pesto myself. The basil grows like weeds back here. I grow the garlic, too. No parmesan, I'm afraid, not until I have a cow." He laughs.

Adam smiles: "Sure."

Pete hands Adam a pot and tells him to make himself useful. "Tap's at the side of the house," he says.

Adam finds it awkward going down the plywood ramp with his new leg. He makes his way gingerly, noticing the cascading basil near the fence, the flowers, the fruit trees, the vines. Pete obviously tends this garden, tames its wilder impulses.

While the water heats up, Pete pulls out a joint, asks Adam if he smokes.

"You grow that yourself, too?"

"Nah. Buddy of mine. I trade him honey for it."

Adam had wondered about the wooden structures at the end of the garden.

"Got the apiary on the left there," Pete points. "Compost, vermiculture bins on the right."

It's enviable, the way the guy has built himself a world. Adam wishes he'd had that kind of resourcefulness in captivity.

Pete passes the joint to Adam. "Marijuana for trauma, man," he says, nodding like some wise old prophet.

He takes the joint from between Pete's stubby fingers. He sucks the smoke in hard, avoiding Pete's eyes. This guy knows, Adam thinks; he knows I am guilty.

"I gotta explain something," Adam slurs into the smoke as he hands back the joint.

"Yeah?"

"There was a kid," he begins.

"Where was this?"

"Somalia."

"Right," says Pete. "Now you're making more sense."

Adam tries to describe the casualty of that last day, but he can hear his speech looping over itself.

Pete wants some clarification: a visual picture. "So say this is you," he says, laying down a spoon. "And here's the kid"—he places a lighter beside the spoon. "And you got this guy over here in the doorway," he says, grabbing a salt shaker. "You got your back to the kid; you say he's propping you up. Well, you don't know what the fuck he's doing, do you? Maybe he's waving his arm, telling them to shoot you. Or maybe he's using you as a shield."

"No," Adam says, shaking his head. "It wasn't like that."

"Ah, come on," says Pete. "You gonna tell me you had some kind of bond with this kid?"

Adam starts shaking his head. He's so high that he can't make himself stop. He closes his eyes and it feels like his brain is liquid sloshing from left to right.

He stumbles out of a cab a couple of hours later. Sofie is sitting on the couch, flicking through the pages of a magazine.

"I went out for drinks with some of the guys in my class," Adam stammers and slumps down into a chair.

"You could have called."

"Sorry," he mumbles.

"I was doing some reading," she says, passing him something she has printed off the internet.

It's a blurry picture of different foods apparently high in sperm-boosting nutrients. She's got a lot more California in her than he ever knew.

Adam hoists himself up with difficulty and weaves toward the bathroom.

"Adam?" she says.

He stops midway down the hall, propping himself against the wall with his elbow and turning around slowly. He raises his palm and says: "Stop, Sofie. Please just stop."

He writes a note later that night, just before he slips away. "I'm sorry I cannot give you what you want, Sofie. You deserve to find it."

LILA

DR. HEINZ ups my dose of antidepressants despite the pregnancy. He's a very practical man, efficient. We don't have the luxury of time but, as he says, we will do our best to clean the house before the baby arrives.

He has me tell him my life story over four sessions, a story that ends with Robin. I feel devastated by the whole shameful mess.

Dr. Heinz barely speaks in these sessions. When I have brought him right up to the present, he leans back in his chair and says, "I think you wanted to be found by a mother. Remembered, longed for, searched for, found."

It's like he is reaching underneath my ribs and pulling out my heart. Like he is holding it in his hands: this red, raw, trembling thing.

Whatever keeps me together falls away. I cry well beyond the end of our hour. It doesn't absolve me of my guilt, but it does allow me to understand some of the complexity of what took place with Robin. I'd seen us both as abandoned children. But I'd kept the clues to where she belonged to myself because *I* did not belong anywhere, to anyone. It is the oldest of wounds.

"I don't matter in that essential way to anyone," I finally whisper to Dr. Heinz.

"You will," says Dr. Heinz, patting his own stomach.

I'm showing by this point, unable to zip up my coat anymore. I don't want to be the pregnant woman at AA so I stop going to weekly meetings. I'm not in any danger of drinking: alcohol, along with coffee and chicken, turns my stomach. Sometimes the body knows best.

The old lady—Marta—brings me a brisket. In fact, she walks straight through my door and into my kitchen and tells me to reheat it for twenty minutes at three hundred and fifty degrees.

"So," she says, leaning in conspiratorially. "Does the father know?"

"I wouldn't worry about him," is all I will give her.

The following week she brings me a handwritten list of all the things her daughter says you need to get when you're having a baby. As intrusive as Marta can be, the list is helpful.

I get myself organized. When Jacqui asks what I need, I refer back to the list.

She and Solomon come by one night with a load of stuff. Jacqui sets Solomon to work building the crib. She wants to talk about how I am set financially, and what I'm planning to do in the future.

"I really think you should have done the review hearing and faced the penalty," she says.

"You can't have people guilty of repeated boundary violations in your profession," I say.

"The penalty, at least, might have helped you forgive yourself."

I'm not sure I deserve forgiveness. "I used her, Jacqui."

"It's not that black and white, Lila. You did ultimately help her. You helped her find her voice."

Yes, but the truth of it is my fantasies required her silence in the larger world.

TESS

I FEEL like I've failed my son. I don't want my child to be lonely. I want him to have a sense of connection to others. I've started looking up questions kids ask about their donors and the possibility of donor siblings, seeking advice about how to formulate thoughtful responses when questions arise. As it is, he's more likely to ask Emily those questions. Somehow I have to find a way to be open to them, and communicate this to Max.

I wonder, and not for the first time, if the donor ever thinks about where his material ended up. Whether he could even imagine the kind of circles that start to form as a result of its dissemination. I have to admit, Emily and I didn't really think through all the implications. I knew there would be other children conceived with the same sperm, but I didn't think of them as people who might one day be curious about or even known to each other.

It's hard to imagine how Max will feel about it all. There's nothing comparable for me to draw from in order to offer him guidance. It's a kind of Wild West out there and he may or may not want us along for the ride. It could be that he'd do better having a sibling growing up alongside him—the certainty of a relationship rather than the vague and complicated promise all this seems to offer.

I'm thinking all this through as I'm driving with some trepidation up to Sudbury in our old car, which Emily has let me borrow this weekend. Unlike me, she had the sense to put her snow tires on in good time, and I know it's better to get back behind the wheel before I become completely paralyzed by the idea of doing so.

It takes just over five hours without stopping. I get to my motel by mid-afternoon. Before I left Toronto, in an effort to be more social, or at least less anti-social, I arranged to meet an acquaintance for a drink tonight, but I'm so preoccupied with other things that I don't think I can do it now.

After sending an apology to Monika I make my way to a pizza place across the road. I pick up a Margherita, returning to my motel room to eat it in all its cardboard glory while sitting cross-legged on the ugly bedspread and flicking on the TV. I fall asleep to reruns of *Law and Order: SVU*.

I pull open the ugly blinds to an ugly grey morning: a few cars in the parking lot, the red signs of the pizza place and a convenience store across the street; behind them, outcroppings of blackened igneous rock. I wonder who stays in a motel like this on the outskirts of an old mining town—who, apart from geographers and men thrown out by their wives?

I feel better in our car, a familiar bubble, with the company of a backdrop of voices on CBC Radio. About half an hour south of Sudbury, I stop for gas in a small town of scattered bungalows with an anglicized French name and a poutine stand boarded up for the next three seasons.

Driving further east, my GPS loses its signal, but there is only one road now, one road with several turnoffs that will take me down to the river. It is only when I get to the shore that I realize the pier and the bridge I have seen in archival photos are no longer there. The religious colony that had been based on the island imploded just over two decades ago, possibly taking the bridge with it.

The island isn't that far from the shore, but the rapids between there and where I'm standing are daunting. The only way to get over there would be by boat, but there's no one out fishing on the river, no Stavros—it's just me and the grey granite and the white spruce leaning with the wind.

I return to the car and drive back to the town, where there will at least be some cell reception and the possibility of a cup of coffee.

Sitting on the picnic table outside the poutine stand I call the only person I know in Sudbury. I apologize again for last night and explain my situation, my stupidity, asking, "You don't by any chance have a boat, do you?" Having come all this way I feel like I am supposed to make a noble effort and try.

"I have a canoe," says Monika.

"Would you be comfortable with me borrowing it?"

"I'm not sure you should cross right there," she says, "at least not alone. I could do it with you tomorrow."

She asks where I'm staying.

"Jesus," she says, when I give her the name of the motel.

"Yeah, maybe not the best choice."

"It's way too rough around there at night," she says, offering to pick me up after her last class today. "I've got a separate apartment over the garage. It's been empty since my daughter went off to McGill."

Monika lives in a warm and rustic log cabin on the edge of town. She builds a fire while I prepare dinner. A carbonara and a green salad. Her dining table is made of a smooth piece of granite shaped like a pear.

"Sudbury's charms aren't immediately apparent, but it is a fascinating place to be a geologist," she says, refilling my glass with red wine.

I point at the various framed family photos propped up on the bookshelf. "It was a busy household," she says. "All girls. Imagine, three of them going through adolescence at the same time—God, they could be savage with each other—but they've turned out to be good people, good to each other, particularly since their dad died."

"I'm so sorry," I say. "How long ago?"

"Three years," she says, running her finger down the stem of her wine glass. "I still wake up sometimes and forget that he's not here."

It's quiet and there's a sadness in the room that I don't know how to alleviate.

"I'm sorry," she says, "I don't mean to bring you down."

"No," I shake my head. "I'm already feeling kind of, I don't know. Heavy. There's a lot going on."

"Do you want to talk about it?" Her face is an open invitation, but the story is complicated, with so many moving parts.

"Why don't you try?" she says, reaching out and squeezing my forearm.

I take a deep breath, then take a clumsy run at it. The pieces start tumbling out, one piling on top of another: Max and Emily, the embryos, the donor, the lawyers, my dad. We've worked our way through a second bottle of wine by the time I get to my mother—and then I'm looping back around again to Emily and Max.

"I didn't understand that her desire to have another child is as much an expression of her love for Max as anything. She has the courage to put him first, to try and give him the sibling he wants, even if that might be really hard for her to do."

"But you understand that now," she says.

I'm absolutely exhausted. It feels like I have just said more to Monika than I did in the entire course of my relationship with Emily.

And then I start to cry. "I'm sorry," I mutter. "I'm not a crier." Monika reaches toward me, pulling me into a hug. My instinct is to pull away, but she holds me there, not letting go.

SOFIE

IT WAS a Friday in the centre of Jijiga, the mosques empty after noon prayers, the streets quiet. The entire town was in repose behind gates and green metal doors. The wheels of my suitcase were clattering over rocks and dirt, drawing the attention of little kids crouched in doorways, undermining my attempts to be inconspicuous in my black Saudi abaya. I was not brown enough and not a woman in the kitchen, preparing or serving food to the men back from the mosque, but a woman wheeling a suitcase full of US dollars down an empty street.

My father had sent the money, refinancing a property he owned in Abu Dhabi. The kidnappers knew exactly who my father was: there was no way to claim I could not gain access to the kind of money they demanded despite the fact that I was paid a local wage in local currency. This is the way I have always been able to maintain my independence from my father. The shame of having to ask him for help felt like a dark heavy thing that would cast a shadow over the rest of my life. It was my fault that Adam was in this situation; I had involved him in the disappearance of those boys. If he were to lose his life, I couldn't have lived with myself. I owed Adam this, but I feared I would end up owing my father even more.

I'd told my father what he needed to hear: this man was my fiancé and I was working with US and UN officials to secure his release. The truth was, my efforts to work through diplomatic channels had been futile.

After Adam had failed to turn up at work for a second day, I had gone to his hotel in Jijiga. The hotel owner had shrugged and snapped his fingers in the air as if to suggest Adam had evaporated. At my insistence, he'd shown me Adam's empty room. I don't know what kind of evidence I imagined I might find. Some sign of his existence, some secret message meant for me. But there was nothing but a fly trapped in a spider's web in a corner of the room.

I immediately went to see Dr. Farhan, the director of camp security, to tell him I thought Daniel had been kidnapped.

"No," said Dr. Farhan, shaking his head. "He's been reassigned."

I almost lost my balance in that moment. "Where?" I stammered.

"Given the nature of his work, that is confidential."

I stood staring at this man, trying to excavate some truth from his face. I realized in that moment that something bigger and much more complicated was going on. Perhaps recruitment for al-Shabaab was happening at the highest levels within the camp. Whatever it was, the director of security was involved.

"That's too bad," I'd said. "It would have been nice to say goodbye. He was a good guy."

"Indeed," Dr. Farhan had said, showing me to the door.

A letter for me arrived three weeks later. No stamps or postmark, just two lines in Arabic about the cost of loving an infidel.

I contacted the US embassy then, from which I received quiet word that the most efficient way to do this would be to hire a private contractor. The US government could not be seen to be negotiating with terrorists.

In return for the money, I promised my father that once Adam was freed, we would move to the US to live the conventional life my parents had always wanted for me. I assured him this would include children. They would have grandchildren once all this was resolved.

I would do what my father had asked and I was doing what the kidnappers had asked—coming alone, lugging two million dollars. Whatever illusion of independence I had been operating under for all these years had been completely shattered. They would behead Adam were I not making my way this late afternoon toward a particular tree that hugged a crumbling whitewashed wall. They would not merely behead him: first they would tie dental floss around his testicles, tugging the ends tighter and tighter until they separated them from his body, ensuring they dropped off "like ripe dates in a shudder of wind," in the Mullah's words.

"Shudder," he had repeated, and it had the effect he intended, cold trickling through me. "And what use then the tree without its fruit?" this man, who fancied himself a poet, then said. "What use your infidel husband to you then?"

My infidel, my Adam, my first man.

I knew I had found the place by the stripe of black paint that ran horizontally across the wall and the trunk of the tree. I waited, as directed, in the shade of its thorns, thorns used to suture the wounds inflicted upon the genitals of women. I know what the tree is called, but I avoid giving it the dignity of a name. It was as if the Mullah had planned every detail in order to signify my subjugation.

A young Somali man in a T-shirt and a long, red-and-purple checkered *macawiis* knotted at the waist approached and leaned against the wall. He stared straight ahead and began issuing directions in Arabic in a voice that wasn't used to its new depth. I turned left as directed, walking down an alleyway littered with broken glass, his breath at my back. I slipped into a narrow entrance between two buildings and he pulled the green metal door closed behind me with a screech, bolting it shut.

A group of men were lounging on a rug in the courtyard, chewing *qat*. The rug was strewn with leaves and stalks, clay cups, a Thermos, packs of Rothmans. The walls surrounding the courtyard were made of clay and corrugated metal and topped with barbed wire and shards of glass. We were in a cage, a prison. There was no way of escape. My pulse was pounding beneath my abaya: I could hear the swoosh of blood in my ears.

"*As-salamu 'alaykum*," said the bearded man at the centre of their prone semicircle. His eyes were hot black coals.

"*Wa 'alaykumu s-salam*," I said demurely, looking at the ground.

"We are glad you could join us," he said. It was the Mullah; I recognized his voice, his English. "Sit," he said, pointing to a corner of the courtyard.

"I have this for you," I said, pushing the suitcase forward. I pulled my shaking hands back into the folds of my abaya.

"Sit," he repeated. "We will count it."

The money was in hundreds. Twenty thousand hundred-dollar bills that had been sent to me from Dubai. The sky above was a thick white haze of heat and I felt crushed on all sides. I crumbled down against the wall, feeling robbed of any agency, knowing I would be there until well after dark.

Asr, Maghrib, Isha'a. With each call to prayer they broke to bow down. I sat still against the wall as the Mullah and his men resumed chain-smoking and counting the US dollars. Finally the Mullah reached two million and then released me unceremoniously into the dark. Relieved as I was to be leaving without incident, I was filled with a sense of dread that something worse awaited me in the street. I made my way cautiously, running my hand against a wall, trying not to stumble over rocks, a dog at my heels. "*Uss, ya kelb*," I kept saying, trying to shoo him.

In the main square, several Somali women were packing up their provisions and stacking them onto their heads for the trek home through the countryside. They stopped and stared as I approached. I was looking for the way to Adam's hotel. There was no way I could get back to the camp at this hour. A woman pulled her son out from behind her *dirac* and patted him on the back. He would show me to the place.

I was forced to jog to keep up with the boy. A few minutes later, he pointed at the entrance and then broke into a sprint.

The hotel owner was holding a flashlight when he opened the door. He beamed it into my face and, seeming to recognize me, ushered me quickly inside. He led me wordlessly up the stairs to Adam's former room and instructed me not to turn on the light. I laid there and for the first time in years, I prayed.

LILA

MARTA COMES by with some soup. She brings it over in a pot that she plunks directly onto my stovetop, then she picks up my sweet Vivian and spits on the floor in order to ward off evil spirits. She sticks a wrinkled stick of a finger into my baby's mouth and walks her around the apartment, all the while giving me unsolicited advice about various aspects of infant care.

I let her prattle on and go about making us some tea.

She is saying that her daughter-in-law tried to teach her grandson sign language when he was a baby and she thought it was crazy, all that time and effort for three words he was going to spit out soon enough.

I sip my tea and look into my baby's dark navy eyes and watch them flutter closed. "I'm going to put her down now," I say to Marta, thanking her for the food.

She gives me reheating instructions before shuffling off, leaving me to lie down with Vivian. Vivian sleeps with me at night despite all the advice against it. "Just trust your instincts," Dr. Heinz says. When I find myself getting drowsy today, I force myself to get up, wanting to cross a few more things off my list.

I send an email to the fertility clinic in order to report Vivian's birth. Then, because my midwife mentioned it the other day, I look up a website for parents of children conceived by way of donor sperm, curious to know if Vivian might have half-brothers and -sisters out there in the world. I enter her donor's ID into their registry and up pops a list of birthdates and birth weights of a number of boys and girls. Thirty-two and counting. It's a little shocking, not just the number, but that this kind of information is right out there in the open, this easy to find.

My own adoption wasn't a secret, but I don't know, for instance, who my mother was beyond some basic facts, and there was never any mention of my father. Perhaps he went on to have other children, perhaps I even have half-brothers and -sisters of my own out there, but I will never know. My daughter will grow up in a very different world, where there is easy access to this kind of information, answers to some of the questions she might have.

There's a noticeboard on the site where a couple of people have posted messages. Apparently there is no more of this donor's sperm available and both of these people are looking for another source. One HappyHippieMama is "hoping for a sibling for the twins!" which strikes me as a little smug and greedy.

The second message, from someone named SoSeeker, is a lot more enigmatic. "Hoping someone can help me. Complicated circumstances. This donor is the only suitable match."

I'm curious as to why this person sees this donor as the only possibility. So curious, in fact, that the question doesn't let me fall asleep. I still have five vials of his sperm, currently doing nothing in a freezer in Atlanta. I could share it, help someone else be a mother.

After feeding Vivian again, I get up and create a profile in order to send a simple message off to SoSeeker in the middle of the night. "I might be able to help you," I write, "but do you mind me asking why this particular donor?"

There is no reply from SoSeeker when I check in the morning. I prop Vivian up in her bouncy seat and turn her to face the piano. It's no grand piano, it's a brown upright given to me by a retiring music teacher. There is an arrow drawn on the wood pointing down to middle C and some lumps of fossilized gum under the bench.

I've started working my way through Bartók's piano cycle *For Children*. The cycle is something of an exercise for students, the pieces increasing in complexity as they go on. I still have the book I bought for Robin, which I will pass on to Vivian if she ever expresses any interest in playing.

In the afternoon, I get Vivian into her car seat, throw the diaper bag over my shoulder and make my way downtown to see my midwife. Vivian is doing well at six weeks, gaining enough weight, and the midwife thankfully gets rid of the last of my stitches.

I'm eager to get home afterwards and check to see if there is a reply yet from SoSeeker, but we're caught in the crawl of rush-hour traffic up Bathurst. I stare out the window at the nannies waiting at bus stops and the Orthodox women in their thick brown wigs and black knee-length skirts, their strollers draped with children. I want to open the window and tell them all that I am a mother, too.

Back at our building, I lug the car seat and the rest of our gear into the elevator, where a man is resting his grocery bag in what used to be Leonard's favourite corner. I think about getting a dog when Vivian is a bit older.

I breastfeed Vivian while I sit at the computer. When I log in to the sibling site, I can see that SoSeeker is currently online. She, or he, has left me a message. "I don't mean to be cryptic," SoSeeker has written, "but can you first tell me whether you have children conceived with his sperm?"

"I do," I write back, seeing no reason not to be honest. "I have a daughter."

"He was my husband," SoSeeker writes back immediately. "He was killed overseas."

Oh my God. I don't know what I'd imagined, but nothing like this.

"I would rather explain it over the phone," she writes.

"Of course," I say, giving her my number.

She writes that she is in Dubai visiting her parents. It is morning there, already forty-two degrees, and her mother is hovering nearby. She will text me when she is more at liberty to speak. Peace, she writes, signing off, *Sofie*.

The next day, as Vivian and I are returning from our daily walk around the neighbourhood, I get Sofie's text. Once we're back in the apartment, I get a glass of water and sit down on the chair in the solarium. She answers on the first ring. She's on the rooftop of her parents' building at sunrise. Her voice is so soft we have to pause for the call to prayer in the background in order for me to hear her clearly.

"I'll answer any questions you have," she says.

But I know enough. "It's okay. I don't need to put you through some kind of interrogation."

"Nobody responded to my post," she says, choking on the words. "It's been up there for months. I know it sounded a bit weird, I must sound a bit weird, but what could I do? I couldn't say I *knew* the donor."

She can barely speak now through her tears. "We were going to have a child; we were trying. But then he had to go away for work, on assignment . . ."

"I'm so sorry, Sofie."

"I can't tell you what it means that you are willing to do this. What can I give you in return?"

This is an act of atonement, but Sofie doesn't know that. I don't need anything, but she is insistent.

"Maybe one day, if my daughter wants to, she can ask you about him, what he was like as a person."

"I can tell you now, if you want."

She might need to tell someone, to talk about this man she has lost, share him with someone, but I am not the right person. I'm likely to construct an idea of him in my mind, project onto him certain characteristics I would find desirable. I need to keep my fantasies out of it.

"You could write a letter to my daughter while your memories about him are still fresh," I suggest. "I'll keep it for when she is ready."

I won't read it. This is for Vivian. I know better than to confuse our stories.

ACKNOWLEDGEMENTS

DEEPEST GRATITUDE to my editor and friend Martha Kanya-Forstner for her wisdom and company through a book that has been a very long time coming.

Thanks to my agent Ellen Levine, and the incredible team at Doubleday Canada for all the work that goes into bringing a book into the world.

Thanks to those who shared their expertise with me on a range of issues affecting my characters' lives. I am grateful to lawyer and social worker Lori Stein for talking to me about children taken into care, to lawyer Sara Cohen for generously guiding me through the complex business of fertility law, and to psychiatrist Lisa Andermann for answering my questions about PTSD.

And finally, big love and thanks to those who have been in the trenches with me throughout: Helene Brodziak, Clare Pain, Mel/Miles Carroll, Diana Bryden, Anne Bayin, Ann Shin, Tammi Gibb and Sheila Fennessy.

CAMILLA GIBB was born in London, England, and grew up in Toronto. She is the author of four internationally acclaimed novels—*Mouthing the Words, The Petty Details of So-and-so's Life, Sweetness in the Belly* and *The Beauty of Humanity Movement*—as well as the bestselling memoir *This Is Happy*. Camilla has been the recipient of the Trillium Book Award, the City of Toronto Book Award and the CBC Canadian Literary Award and has been shortlisted for the Scotiabank Giller Prize and the RBC Taylor Prize. She has a Ph.D. from Oxford University and is an adjunct faculty member of the graduate creative writing programs at the University of Toronto and the University of Guelph.